Confessions of an Italian Priest

LINNEA NILSSON

SKITTISH
ENDEAVOURS ™

LINNEA NILSSON

Confessions of an Italian Priest

A SKITTISH ENDEAVOURS BOOK:

Originally published in Great Britain by Skittish Endeavours 2023
Copyright © Linnea Nilsson 2023, All Rights Reserved
First Edition

The right of Linnea Nilsson to be identified as the author of this

work has been asserted in accordance with sections 77 and 78 of the Copyright Designs and Patents Act 1988.

Conditions of Sale

Skittish Endeavours Books are supplied and printed by Amazon

Printed and bound by Amazon at www.amazon.com

Thanks to:-

Design Sara Mitchell of Techflame LLC.

Copy Editor: Dee Groocock of Stellar Reads

For more information on Linnea Nilsson see her Facebook Page at

https://www.facebook.com/LinneaNilsson

INDEX

CHAPTER 1

I had chosen the wrong life.

I was locked in the confessional, keeping myself busy guzzling a Corona, complete with lemon tucked into the neck of the bottle. That song kept running through my head without interruption, *Hit the road, Jack*, and the idea of not coming back no more was quite appealing.

The habit of isolating myself further, usually in the early afternoon, and taking out a carton of beer before the afternoon mass, was a tradition I started after a particularly difficult exorcism years before. Still, I was doubtful if it succeeded or not. Not that I knew of other priests respecting this orthodoxy, as much as I was aware, beer was my thing alone. Of course, others would bend an elbow with *vin santo*, but those were mostly of the old guard.

No, nothing better than a cold beer. I also wanted to smoke but the smell would have stank the confessional. I tried it once and the nuns had launched dirty looks in my direction all the time. I even attempted to smoke the Swiss cigarettes, which smelled of incense. Another failure, I could have smoked a joint in the first place, but that afternoon I had no desire to climb up to the top of the Bell Tower.

"Father Venanzio, Father Venanzio!" shouted a boy's voice. I heard the heavy footsteps, in a hurry, as he approached. I drank one last mouthful from the bottle, I rested it on the ground and I popped my head out from the confessional.

"What's up, George?" I asked the young boy who had just entered. His glasses were far too big for his face.

"The guys on the pitch are beating the crap out of each other", said the boy. He was short of breath.

A wasted beer, I thought, but I rose, following the youth outside the Church. I hadn't yet walked ten steps when another voice called to me.

"Father Venanziooo ..."

Gosh! What a shithole this town was, Bareggio. If they didn't have a priest around all the time they couldn't move a bloody finger. What a bunch of idiots. I turned around, putting on the best smile I had in my repertoire and said "Simonetta! How can I help you? "

"I have sinned, father, I must confess".

I stood there for a moment in silence, considering the two options. On one hand I would have happily watched a fight between boys, on the other hand I had Simonetta with her sins. Simonetta had started coming to church recently and each time her sins were erotic dreams, which I swept away with a couple of Hail Marys; but I had to confess, the woman in that moment seemed the best of the two options considering also the half beer I had left in the confessional. What should I have done?

The bespectacled boy looked at me imploringly, but the decision had been taken. "I'm sorry George. Confessions take precedence out of an oratory's fight. Aren't they playing rugby anyway? Fighting is part of the sport, it revitalises" and then returning my attention to the woman waiting I said, "follow me to church."

Worst case scenario, there were at least three beers to finish.

I put on the regalia and entered the confessional; the woman, kneeling, was already saying "bless me, father, for I have sinned." Me too, I thought.

I made the sign of the cross with the bottle of Corona, I gobbled one more sip and I started to listen.

Simonetta was in her thirties. Hair cut in a bob, fake blonde, and particularly attractive:

she was petite and skinny, but not too much. From the notes the old pastor left, I knew Simonetta was not adept at showing up in church. Just occasionally visiting at Easter and Christmas. Her conversion began when I had moved to Bareggio.

"And how did you sin, Simonetta?" I asked.

"I had impure thoughts", the woman hurried to answer.

"Please do tell me, my daughter." I had to smile. If I was the father then logically all parishioners were daughters, even the fossilised 80 year olds. Or sons, but I had a preference for daughters. Despite her young age, I couldn't be the father anyway. I was thirty-five myself and barring an unlikely miracle, biology was not an option. I could be the father of her children though.

"It all happened tonight. Or rather yesterday. I mean I dreamt last night, but about something that happened yesterday in the office."

Jesus Christ, she liked to natter. Before she could get to the point, she made you suffer throughout the confessions. Never once did she say "I dreamt about a nice big cock, under the guise of a serpent, who was sneaking between my thighs." No, she had to spell out the details, the foreplay, the motivations.

"Do you want to start from the dream or the antecedent?"

"The what?" said Simonetta astonished.

"From what happened yesterday." Holy patience.

"Oh that one. Yes of course. I told you I work at Tecnamatic, right? I'm a secretary, and believe me when I say that place is a jungle!"

"Tecnamatic is the one that makes printing machinery, right?" I asked curiously.

"Oh, but they do not just do that, the dirty pigs. Behold, yesterday I went to the basement, where the archives are housed. I was there to retrieve some old documents for my boss, and didn't I hear all that panting behind a door?"

Here we go, I thought, unaware at that point that the thing would go far longer, "And what did you do?"

"Well, Father Venanzio, there and then I thought maybe it was one of the workers, who maybe had an asthma attack. You know, if it happens down there in the basement it is big trouble. Nobody is going to find you in the midst of all those shelves. Mind you, what a worker was doing in the archives was a mystery that I hadn't yet solved, but at that time I decided not to ask.

"Always help those in need, thus sayeth the Lord," I replied while trying to uncap another Corona without making too much noise.

"That's what I thought too. But then I realised the moans seemed to belong to two different people, and so I opened the door slightly. I'm not telling you what my poor eyes saw!"

I tried to do the math quickly: sneak peek at two making love, two Lord's Prayer and three Hail Marys. Subsequent wet dream, two more Hail Marys. I actually should have taken into consideration the licentiousness of the dream, the subject's involvement, impure deeds, but at that time I was busy opening a new bottle and it didn't seem appropriate to complicate the matter further. I wrapped the bottle in my robe, gave it a tug, and finally the bottle opened, but the sudden movement made me spill part of the precious nectar.

"Jesus Christ!"

Simonetta, believing that the curse was aimed at her, continued, "Exactly my own reaction. That's why I came to confess."

"Continue please," I said trying to dry the soaked robe with the stole.

"As I said, I was peeking. And what I saw was Galbiati, pants down, who was making love to a woman from the marketing department.

"Galbiati had his back to the door or was he sideways?" never leave out the details: if mister Galbiati was presenting his back to the door then I would have to delve into how Simonetta could recognize him. On the other hand, if Galbiati was seen from the side he could have shown the family jewels and in that case maybe I should have also added another couple of Hail Marys.

"He was in profile. At first, I did not recognise who the female was, but then I saw her well and it was Mariapina from the marketing department. They were banging like a shithouse door in a storm, Father Venanzio. Pardon me for the expression. He was taking her from behind and she was moaning and bouncing. She has breasts like volley balls. Galbiati had his thing hard and straight and he did not pray to shove it in full length. I didn't know that cocks could be that big, and Galbiati is so skinny; no one would say at first glance that under his pants he had such a sledgehammer."

"And then?"

"And then I got wet with excitement and I started touching myself. Oh my Gosh, I'm wet as well now, just by telling you all this. And it's hot. Father Venanzio isn't it hot staying in the confessional all day in this warm weather?"

"Not really, I have a portable fan to keep me cool", I replied. And an icy Corona. "Why don't you come in here to confess? At least you can enjoy some fresh air."

"But can I? I've never seen anyone go in there except the priests."

"It's not the place that matters, but the confession and the repentance at the end."

Simonetta stood up and walked to the entrance of the confessional. She opened the wooden door, looked around for a brief moment to make sure no one could see her on that sultry afternoon, then she drew back the curtain and entered.

"Certainly, you have a nice place here," she said, looking around as if she were studying a nave, "I understand why you spend all day in here. A bit tight though."

"The original idea was to separate the sinner from the representative of God. The sinner must suffer on the knees as a sign of humility before the Lord; on the other side the priest who has no reason to be uncomfortable."

"I mean, am I kneeling in here?"

"No, those are things of the past. Here, you

can sit here on my legs," I said by patting my hands on my thighs. Thinking about it for a moment, having her on her knees would have not been a bad idea after all, but it was too late. Never speak without first thinking was what they always taught in Seminary. Simonetta turned back and after a few twerking movements of her arse she got comfortable and settled. All that sweeping began to take effect. "Please continue," I said.

"Yes, I was saying ... I was wet and so I started to touch myself. Could you believe how ashamed I would have felt if someone had caught me in the act. I was outside the door with a hand between my legs whilst Galbiati had his big stick between the legs of Mariapina banging her like a shit house door."

I felt the warmth of Simonetta against my body. It was almost summer, she wore a denim dress, short enough, two beautiful tapered legs were scratching mine at every movement. Simonetta was not tall, but those legs were slender and well proportioned, especially when close at hand. I put the half-finished Corona on the floor. That movement triggered her to sway slightly, causing more friction. Gosh, I was excited myself. I grabbed her thighs to keep her from slipping away. Only when I was again settled down did I slip my hands down the sides, of that short skirt made of denim, and I reached her thighs. They were smooth and firm, as expected.

For a moment I was afraid that she would ask "Father Venanzio, is it the sprinkler that you have in your pants or are you pleased that I came to confess? " I wouldn't have known what to answer, but instead Simonetta continued to tell her story.

"Mariapina was lying on the boxes and I saw all that flesh dancing around back and forth, like when you shake the panna cotta in the pot to check the texture. Do you know that she has a little cellulite? Well, at that point Galbiati got up and made her lay on one side. I wasn't expecting that from Galbiati, he is always so shy and instead on that occasion he was pushing her like an obsessed man. All red in the face and he moved like an eel. But you know, Father Venanzio, that Galbiati has a monster cock between his legs?"

"Yes, you have already said that."

"At that point I was dripping wet and I slipped a finger inside me."

I pushed my hand under her skirt and I reached her panties. Simonetta kept her legs slightly apart and let me do whatever I wanted. Finally, a respectable parishioner. After weeks of confessions that gave me the mother of all boners at least she had the decency of not backing out.

"Even now you seem excited", I said feeling the wetness on my fingertip.

"Father Venanzio, if you saw what I saw, those two at work shagging like rattlesnakes, you would be excited too. It was like watching a blue movie."

"How many have you watched so far? You didn't mention about this before."

Caught red-handed, Simonetta paused, perhaps to find a suitable excuse, but then went on the attack: "You seem excited too. Look, don't you think I can feel that hard knob you have between your legs pushing against my butt?"

"What can I say, Simonetta. Sometimes the flesh is weak; we are sinners and temptation makes us do things we regret. But our Lord in his infinite goodness forgives us." At that point I was masturbating her openly and the parishioner had definitely lost concentration. With some difficulties I unzipped my pants. Holding her hips I pushed her against my hardened cock and made my way in. It entered without resistance, she was hot, tight as I liked and the operation was accompanied by a sigh from both of us.

"And then how did it end, with those two?"

"I didn't hang around waiting for them to finish. At one point I came, I pulled up my panties and I ran to the office. I was lucky I wasn't caught because I had a loud orgasm. I couldn't do anything about it, I had to scream."

It wasn't going to take long before I had the chance to hear it myself, I held onto her by her hips and pumped with as much enthusiasm as I had in my body and Simonetta was following my movements with some of her own. She put her hands on the confessional walls so she could push better against me and she panted hard. She came first and I had to put my hand over her mouth because she was making a mess with her "ahhhh!" and "I'm coming". Anyone who had walked into the church at that moment would have thought I was dealing with an exorcism gone wrong and for sure would run away like hell. A few more strokes and I came too. I didn't ask if she was on the pill, but it was better not to risk it. The gush of semen ended on the dividing curtain, leaving a stain that was taking the shape of a weeping Redeemer. I created my very own sacred Shroud.

Simonetta pulled up her panties, she sat on top of me and heaved a sigh. "Now I have another sin to confess!"

"Don't worry, I'll give you a comprehensive penance."

"But now do you have to confess too?" she asked worried.

"Probably, even if the Lord in his infinite glory has already forgiven me. Two Hail Marys and three Lord's Prayers."

Simonetta thanked me and was going to exit. "You never told me about the dream," I asked.

She turned to me with a mischievous smile and said, "I dreamt that we were making love in the confessional." And then she disappeared in a hurry.

Where the fuck had I left my beers?

CHAPTER 2

"May I come in?"

"Sure, come in, Peter, I'm not doing anything interesting." Peter Oguntoye was a routine visitor. A Nigerian who survived by selling fake handbags and improbable Rolex watches near the Milan central station. Every evening he came back to Bareggio where he shared an apartment with a dozen compatriots; a Northern League militant would have said hundreds. Peter had a story out of the ordinary: he was raised in England, and he had even studied at Oxford with a scholarship. His parents, irregular immigrants, worked like dogs to make him study but, due to the British bureaucracy and the immigrant hunt, carried out with meticulous precision as only the British can do, they had been expelled in a hurry. Such were the English people, loyal to retain the status quo. To guarantee privileges and benefits to the natives but then furiously go after those who really worked. The UKIP was getting increasingly more popular by the day, as in Italy, the Northern League. A nation who used tradition to mask lack of imagination and little desire to work.

"Did you come here to bum another meal?" I asked.

"Of course, wasn't it you folk who invented all that bullshit about the good Samaritans? Now you pay the consequences."

"Come on, sit down. I have pork stew on the stove, unless you prefer the rolls of ham."

"Certainly for a priest, you're an asshole!" said Peter pulling a chair from under the table and sitting down in front of me. He seemed particularly interested in my Sunday sermon.

"And you, with your Ramadan, you are also full of bullshit, aren't you? You can eat in the period of the night in which you can't tell apart a white wire from a black one, or some shit like that. If you think about it, it means that your God can't see in the dark, so how does he know if you eat pork or lamb?"

"The story about the pig and wiping one's arse with ones left hand has nothing to do with Ramadan, which marks the ninth month of the year. Fucking hell, don't they teach you anything in this shitty country?"

As a matter of fact he was not wrong. Indoctrination was an integral part of Christianity. Come to think of it, every religion. "Oh well, then I'll see what I have in the fridge, leave the stew for tomorrow. Are you sure you don't want to taste a bit of prosciutto di Parma? You don't know what you're missing. By the way, today I cleaned my butt with my right hand, just to get you out of spite."

"And this would be the bullshit you say to your faithful people?" he said ignoring my provocation and resting the sermon again on the table.

"That's last year's sermon, tomorrow I'm going to reuse it, nobody will notice. One of these days I will do a social experiment, I'm going to change the Gospel and see if anyone notices."

I got up to rummage in the fridge. There was still half a lasagne left by the *perpetua*. "Lasagne or beef steak? I'll put on some fried potatoes with rosemary, ok?"

"The lasagne is fine, if it's the same as she prepared last time."

Alessia, the *perpetua*, had hands of gold. She came to see me every single morning and cooked for hours without ever asking for anything in return. It was a thing of the past, Father Martian (actually his name was Marzio, but he was so out of this world that the nickname seemed appropriate) had her cooking sauces and roasts for all his life and had become fatter than a monk. Now he was retired and he had gone back to his village near Asiago leaving the vacancy for me.

"The very same. Half an hour to heat it up and we are ready." I opened a bottle of Barolo Riserva Monfortino and filled two glasses. I put one in front of my guest, who sniffed it like a connoisseur before he guzzled the nectar.

"Maybe instead of the Gospel you should edit something else, like the responsorial psalm: ' the Lord's grace is forever: may thee stay hard forever," said Peter.

"Careful with that kind of statement. If you get caught by the Northern League saying something like that, they are gonna cut off your big, black salami and hang it on the outskirts of the city as a warning to other 'non-EU immigrants'."

"Where are the white women?" he said placing a hand on his family jewels.

"Ahahaha! Wrong profession for that, you should have been a milkman or a plumber. Even those are working on the sly like you do."

Peter drank another sip of Barolo and then pushed the glass back in the middle of the table. The universal language to say that it was time for another dose of holy spirit.

"Wait, I have an idea--" I said after filling

both glasses. I walked up to the shelf of books and after a short consultation I found what I was looking for. "Here you are: from the book of Ezekiel *'You also took the fine jewellery of gold and silver I had given you, and you made male idols with which to prostitute yourself.'* That is, they were even making expensive dildos at that time. Do you sell any of those or just fake Rolex? I'm not inventing, it's a quote from Isaiah,"

'And Israel will take possession of the nations and make them male and female servants in the Lord's land.

They will make captives of their captors and rule over their oppressors by subjugating their butts and will dominate their opponents with blows of lashes on the back.'

"Are you making that up?" asked Peter.

"No, just some minor altering: *"On the day the Lord gives you relief from your suffering and turmoil and from the harsh labour forced on you, for you will take up this taunt against the king of Babylon:*
How the oppressor has come to an end!
How his fury has ended!
The Lord has broken the rod of the wicked."

"Come to think about it, it doesn't seem to need any changing at all," said Peter.

"Wait, it ain't over 'til it's over: *"I will sit enthroned on the mount of Venus,*

I will ascend above the tops of the clouds;

I will make myself like the Most Big in the groins

and you will be brought down to the realm of the dead,

Where you will suffer the beating of my lash."

"Now you are definitely inventing. Fifty shades of Isaiah!"

"Amen, brother" I said jingling my glass against his.

"Listen, I appreciate you are feeding me lasagne, but how about buying a nice Rolex? It looks real, you cannot see any difference from an original one, and it makes the same tick tock as the real ones, not those rubbish copies which work on batteries. One hundred euro."

I always liked Rolexes but I was allergic to nickel. All it took was a metal watch, or the buckle of a belt against the skin to trigger an allergy. "I'm sorry, Peter, but the faithful would not understand. Would you donate to charity during Sunday mass to a priest wearing a Rolex on his wrist?"

"In America they are not that fussed, it is full of soul shepherds doing television sermons and driving a Rolls Royce. You're the last priest with morals."

That I wasn't so sure about, but in a small town like Bareggio appearance was everything. "I tell you what, I'll buy a couple of bags from you and put them in the raffle on Sunday. And then don't complain we are the infidel ones ..."

"Thanks, Venanzio."

"And don't give me a Louis Vuitton, everybody has one nowadays and they are all fake no matter what."

"Hermes?"

"Too expensive. Nobody in a sane state of mind would give it to the church, they are usually kept in a bank."

He began to look in his duffel bag. "Gucci and Trussardi."

"They're perfect."

"I'll give you a special price."

Probably not, but with Peter I wouldn't barter. With any of them, to be honest.

It was time to serve the lasagne, which we ate in religious (each one in their own way) silence.

CHAPTER 3

I had been in the waiting room for over an hour when the secretary came calling me: the bishop would finally receive me. I got up reluctantly, I would rather stay in that waiting room and admire the fabulous artwork, which adorned the walls. So, I had always imagined a representative office, and by representing our Lord, maker of all things visible and invisible, this could not be more glitzy.

The Bishop, Father Filiberto, did not get up from the desk, but he just nodded to invite me to sit. Bad sign. He was busy reading a huge computer printout like trying to steal secrets as you do with the cabal, the numbers were the ultimate truth. Receipts, bank statements, phone records of the municipality on revenue from secondary urbanisation works. By law every town had to give a contribution to the church whenever some new building was erected. Plus, people could make an eight thousand percent donation to the church, tax deductible. God was also hiding in those papers.

In the meanwhile, I was lost observing the nuances in the huge rooted wood desk, I was following the lines, trying not to think about the reprimand that inevitably would come soon.

When he was satisfied with the numbers, he began to tinker on the computer, writing totals and who knows what else. Hosanna in Excel Sheet Deo.

He turned off the screen and looked me straight in the eye. "Father Venanzio, I am really disappointed. I wouldn't have expected this from you!"

Here it was coming, I thought.

"Did you really believe that we would not know? We're not idiots; two thousand years of history and any priest newcomer thinks they know better than all of us put together, only to change his mind at the end."

The Bishop was grim-faced and when things did not go according to his expectations, he seemed even more gaunt and skeletal than he already was. He must have been about 60 years old, badly worn, short hair with a military cut, skeleton hands that grasped objects like claws, elongated face with hollow cheeks and a nervous tic in his left eye that made his face wrinkle causing him to appear as though he had a constant grimace. That tic drew attention, people could not avert their gaze from it. As with fire, it fascinated them. And that was the risk with the Bishop: people would keep watching all those twists of muscles and forgot to listen to what the old man was saying. And then they would pay the price for their inattention.

"I'm sorry, your Holiness."

"I'm not the Pope, your Excellency is fine," he said. It was clear from the tone he used that his career was not going according to his expectations.

"You would be a great candidate, in my humble opinion."

"Sure, sure, over time that might happen. But that's not why I made you come here." He paused as long as a mass, then reopened the computer printouts and continued, "It's the second quarter in a row that you did not reach the quota, Father Venanzio, and the previous quarters are not much better. How the heck are you handling your parish? The accounts are clear."

"The donations in this period were less than expected. You know, the crisis." I wasn't going to tell him bullshit about the roof having to be redone, those were excuses for newbies. It was fine to use it as an excuse to ask the sheep to open their wallets, but it would not work with a hungry wolf like the Bishop. "And I am working with the boys in the oratory. I mentioned to you about the rugby team. This year we are enrolling in the rugby championship and we also plan to win it. The equipment was paid for by a sponsor, so on that front we are covered. I hope to attract the new generation and make them like the sport. An investment for the future."

"Yes, those are all laudable initiatives, but my job is to think about today. What you have collected so far is below expectations. You must persuade your parishioners to donate more. This year we all have more ambitious goals, eight per cent more than last year. We're trying to keep the Church alive here, the Western culture is at risk and we need money. Always."

"To remind our faithful about the dictates of Christ the Redeemer. Poverty, charity and hope." I said tentatively. Keep them poor and ignorant, let them open their wallet with any possible excuse and ... hope. I never understood it was the hope that they didn't become aware of what we were doing to them or the hope that what they gave us was going to do good for somebody. More likely the hope of earning a few stitches in front of the judgment of our Lord, a small discount on wrongdoings that we all did on a daily basis."

"Exactly, you see? You know those things, Father Venanzio, now you have to put them into practice!"

"Competition is fierce" I threw out there and I almost laughed in his face. On the contrary the Bishop seemed to ponder that statement.

"Their marketing is better than ours."

On that there was little doubt. He continued, "You see, Venanzio, that idea of the burka is a stroke of genius. When a Christian goes around it is not evident to which religion they belong. You see a guy in a suit and tie or a woman in a business suit and you think 'professionals'. Jeans and t-shirt? Same speech, could be baristas, painters, bankers, teachers, nobody thinks about what religion they belong to, apart from the occasional crucifix exposed on the chest. Whereas those Muslims? Any woman who goes around with the chador, the first thing you think is, *'here's a Muslim'*. Each person is the carrier of the message. And that story in the news about the burkini? It went in all the papers. The French did right by banning it. Those Muslims do not stop at anything in order to make proselytes, we should learn."

"A holy war is long overdue, that would

bring back the attention to our field. I mean, the last time people were interested in us was in the seventies with the working priests, then nothingness." By now I was roller coasting.

"Don't tell me, I've been saying for years that we should get more involved with the armed forces and the military, but the Popes nowadays have no backbone. They all pursue peace talks because it seems to be the right thing to do, but in the end, it is not going to pay off. Just look at those of ISIS and it soon becomes clear that we were wrong in our strategy."

We had a product to sell, we were marketing manager, sales, the homilies were infomercials. Anything to keep the boat afloat.

"If we are not going to war against the Muslims then the only alternative is technology," I said. That gave him something to think about.

"Maybe, but we can't go on posting on Facebook. There is a risk that someone too eager misplaces a comment and goodbye, the post goes viral and we lose more faithful. Sometimes it is better to shut up."

"No, I was thinking about something else. I was talking last month with the parish priest of Cernusco. What we need is a nice App to keep on the phone. If no one comes to church, then having an App makes sense. Confess your sins on your phone and the App dispenses you with a couple of Hail Marys. Your sins are forgiven."

The Bishop was not convinced. "But then they are no longer coming to Church."

"They are not coming anyway. Think about it, first of all we create a nice database of loyals, emails, credit cards etc. Over time we populate the App with the most common sins and four clicks away the confession is made. Then we set a daily message, as a reminder "Did you confess today?" It is going to be like a Tamagotchi. For a few minutes a day we keep the faithful glued to religion, every single day."

The Bishop was not very conducive to technology, especially when it meant investing money. "But if there is no repentance ..." he tried to argue.

"If you log in, it is because you already have repented, don't you think? Otherwise, they would continue to play Angry Birds. Then we could put some paid features in the App, for example, you committed blasphemy five euro, an adultery thirty euro, an abortion ..."

"You must be joking, Venanzio, you know very well that abortion cannot go on that list!"

"Just with blasphemy, in Tuscany, we would make millions. Maybe we reintroduce the plenary indulgences, ten years off purgatory for two hundred and fifty euro. We are all sinners."

The Bishop was a traditionalist, I would have to tread carefully otherwise he would have asked for an App in Latin. "And then the parish priest of Cernusco has contacts in Hewlett Packard, they have a computer monitoring software that shows how many users are logged on, when, what they did, etc. We could do a number of mailing lists, the possibilities are endless, as are the ways of the Lord."

"Okay Venanzio, do me a project plan and a Gantt chart, and I want the costs in detail, if I have to expose this idea to the Monsignor. Let's do a pilot in your parish and then we decide on a national roll-out. Maybe worldwide ..." You could see the big bucks reflected in those lynx eyes, but still I wasn't out of the woods.

"It goes without saying that if it turns out to be a fiasco, your rank will go backward. If I also consider the numbers of your last two quarters then ..."

"What are you going to do, send me to Aspromonte?"

"No way! Those are first level parishes, you have to do a lot of apprenticeship before you get there. With all the mafiosi and camorristi that are there, the church donations are always hearty. That would be far above of your skills. Where there is sin, there must also be us to save those poor souls."

And make money in the process, I thought.

"If you mess this up I shall send you to Riccione. That is a land of the communists and tourists, neither of these categories go to church. A life of misery."

I looked at his black tailored suit, smooth and soft and made to order, golden rings, and I couldn't avoid the comparison with my black jacket and shirt, bought at the local market.

Riccione would not have been the worst of all punishments.

Before he sent me back to the parish, he gave a final warning, "and remember about abstention."

Thinking about Simonetta, I sighed, "the woman is the one sent by the devil, I remember it well."

"What the fuck are you talking about, Venanzio. The abstention! There is the referendum next Sunday. Remember parishioners are to vote no or to abstain. If they change the Constitution, these Communists, can make any crap they want and get away with it. Also take away the eight per thousand donation to the church. The status quo should remain. Now go, I've already wasted too much time with you."

"Praise the Lord."

"May He always be praised."

The town building commissioner was sitting on the same stool that I had occupied in the waiting room one hour before. He admired, open mouthed, paintings and statues. The Lord cannot be commanded, we obey the Lord.

CHAPTER 4

On one thing the Bishop was right, I had to scrape together more money if I didn't want to see myself in trouble. Not that Riccione was the worst of evils, indeed. But when you went into someone's crosshairs, someone so powerful as the Bishop, it was necessary to do everything to go back to normality, to become again the grey man, the one nobody paid attention to.

With the homilies and offerings at church I wouldn't have gone anywhere. The weekday morning masses were depressing: four old-timers at best, a pair of Albanians who come to church every now and then to take relief from the scorching sun, sometimes they even eat breakfast on a bench inside. Better than eating in the street.

I had to knock door-to-door, walking every building and villa in the district and begging. Blessing of the cars? By now there were two or three per family, five euro a pop like a travel insurance, it was June then and the holiday season was approaching.

A nice top-up of the blessing of the House, even if for that, in theory, I shouldn't ask anything and hope for an offer. Yes, Venanzio, the one living in hope dies crapping, well before reaching the quarterly quota fixed by the Bishop. Not to consider my parishioners were a bunch of scrooges, they would give me pennies at best. At the end of a ride, I'd returned home with an ounce of shrapnel in my pockets, the equivalent of twenty euro. They had money to buy mobile phones, that was for sure, the bastards, but to save their souls? Maybe a euro once in a while. I didn't blame them. And nobody was scared about the devil anymore, thanks to Hollywood who had jumped on the bandwagon of the Marvel movies. Long gone were the good times of movies like the Exorcist and the horror films made in the eighties. Too bad, because the devil was real, I saw it with my own eyes and still I had the chills thinking about it.

That would have been enough motivation to get back on the right track but every time I thought about it, I had got the heebie-jeebies and I held fast to the bottle. Here, a Corona was just what I needed to get some fresh ideas.

I took one out of the fridge, the last one, and as soon as I took a sip, without lemon, I had an idea. I guzzled the Mexican in one gulp and ran to the oratory as if they'd put a habanera chilli in my behind. I would have won the

Grand National, if I were a horse.

"George, I need to talk to you," I said to the bespectacled nerd that hung around the oratory as if he didn't have anything else to do with his life. He was sort of a lieutenant, a Templar in the making that helped me with the rugby team. A wholehearted sentinel who stood guard at the gasoline drum in a deserted oratory. The boy was on the route to hermitage without knowing it. He should have been a skirt-chaser at that age, shagging like a rattlesnake, catching gonorrhoea to keep hidden from his parents. Instead, he stood alone. He would have endured the price during the years to come; I made up my mind to do something about it, but not at that moment.

"All right, Father Venanzio?"

"Sure, sure. You are good with computers, right?" I asked suddenly and immediately I regretted it, he was not suitable for what I had in mind but the die was cast.

"A bit, why?" he asked.

"I shall need to make a website. Soon."

"Is it for the Church?" he asked with a twinkle in his eye. Some people had their true own vocation.

"Special project for the Bishop," I lied.

"If you have time we can work on it now," his hand ran to the bag he was carrying, as a Gunslinger in the wild west goes for his trustworthy Colt. "I've got my tablet!"

We set off towards the room where we had the games, table tennis, table football, strictly empty at that time in the afternoon. Some would arrive later, but not many.

George took out the tablet and a keypad and began to tinker. "We can use Wix or Go Daddy which are ready made sites. Do you have a domain yet?"

Maybe. The Emperor of Bareggio, his Holiness Venanzio Vavasour of hinterland, the emperor of San Vittore Olona. This is my domain. I asked him "A domain?" Wrong question because good George began to explain. Hell, I hadn't thought about which name I should give the website.

I reasoned about it for a moment. The good Catholics would open the purse but only for a distant cause. They were pretty pissed off with the Africans, the Moroccans, the Indians, the Pakistanis, the Syrians, sailors, traffickers and refugees. Those were already pleading to them every single day, in front of the supermarket, outside the church, on every corner of the street. They knew their stuff, there was no denying it. The beggars ambushed them outside of the stores, when they were most vulnerable. Nothing in the world makes you as upset as someone who asks you for money for a sandwich when you've just been shopping for the entire week or when you bought a pair of shiny new shoes for two hundred euro.

No, they wouldn't want to hear about local miseries. People help the poor if they're at home, in their own messed up countries. You gladly give a few euro to clear your conscience as long as they don't come here busting our balls. But for a cause far away, it could be done. There are plenty of people adopting whales and Bengal Tigers from a distance without blinking, and forking money in the process. The Middle East was dangerous ground in a Northern League stronghold. Too much hate. Better to focus on Africa. With Africa nothing was going to go wrong, ever.

And children with swollen bellies and desperate eyes.

"Project Oasis" was about to be born, a small donation to give water to a large group of brats. In the heat of June, people would take the bait.

"Do we put a free domain or do you want something specific, like progetto-oasi.com?"

asked George.

"What's the difference?"

"The first smells of a homemade job, with a custom domain it looks more like a professional initiative. But it costs a hundred euro."

"Go with a custom domain."

"And pictures, which ones are we going to use?" my expert continued.

"Download some from Google, some poor and malnourished child and stick them on the front page. And maybe a few African children in front of a school. Those would be the kids already helped by the initiative," I said.

"Ah, but then the initiative is already underway? Anyway, you can't, those images have copyright, you get in trouble if they catch you. If you don't have original photos about the initiative, we must get some from a site that authorises ..."

As if I wasn't already in trouble. "Okay, okay. How much is it going to cost me?"

"Seven euro per photo. Here are some examples," he said opening a stock photos website, having researched a bit. I chose a dozen pics. Shit! I was already at a loss and would have to pay out of my pocket. That loan shark of the Bishop would have surely noticed the unauthorized expense from the church account and would have asked pointed questions. He would not take lightly a charitable initiative that did not exist.

George worked on the site for a bit longer and eventually the site was ready and online. With credit card payment and bank account of the parish.

"Two things, George. First of all the view count. We are at one. Can you change to thirty-five thousand and put a visible counter?"

"Why?"

Because I was asking, for fuck's sake, that's why. "People are more inclined to do something if other people have already done it. And could you could put a counter on donations also? Let's start from 15,000 euro."

"That is illegal and also a bit too complicated. We should ..."

"George, for once, do whatever the fuck I tell you and you will see that it will open the doors of the Kingdom of heaven for you. For fuck's sake, we are not robbing Fort Knox, it is a charitable initiative. And I need printed pages."

"What's the point? you can see the site directly from the phone ..." objected the boy.

"George, if you want to piss me off you're on

the right track. Trust me." I couldn't go to some God-fearing people and show a site on a tablet or a mobile phone. Rule number one: if you were going to ask for money you had to be poorer than the parishioners. How many times I've heard *they cry poverty but they have a television*, aimed at poor folks. As if the telly was some kind of luxury. Or the irritation of seeing immigrants with cell phones: "*They have phones that are better than mine. Like hell I'll give them some money.*" Maybe that phone was the only link that poor people had with family at home. Peter saved on eating to do a top up on his phone and call his family in Nigeria regularly. He was living a shitty life but at least he had a chance to tell his parents some bull story, saying that everything was fine and there was nothing to worry about, that he would be back soon, that he would have made a fortune in Italy. I had seen so many who had lived a life of shit just to be able to pay for a meal for their family back in Africa. Doing slave jobs in the hope of sending their children to school, trying to give them the chance of a decent life.

No, a printout would have been perfect and I would have written the website name with a pen.

"Another thing, George. Make me a copy of this website but keep it offline. And we are even going to put pictures of the parents. Behold, go back on that stock photos website and pick up some of those tribes showing their cocks, those with the spout on the penis."

"Those are in Papua, New Guinea."

"Then some other tribes, as long as we can see their jewels. And some beautiful black girl with long legs and nice juicy breasts, perhaps with a baby in her arms."

George had now realized that it was useless to argue. He raised an eyebrow but started looking. The guy seemed to prefer the brawny girls and I could not disagree on that.

About adding the big men with big dicks, that was going to be my task, I just had the right idea.

When the job was done, George looked at the site with a satisfied look on his face. He was rightly proud, he had done a fine job.

"We need some content, like articles on the initiative and so on," he said.

"Don't worry, I'm on it" I did all right with words, maybe I could have recycled one of my sermons.

"And remember to update the donation counter every night," he said. Clever boy.

"Thanks, you did a bang-up job. Here, these are the keys to the oratory movie theatre. Ask young Carletto to explain to you how it works and bring your friends to the movies whenever you want. Or some girlfriend. You'll see the movie premiere. The key also opens the audiovisual room in the library, I recorded all the Six Nations matches, the All Blacks. And other stuff."

He took the key without saying a word, but I could tell he was pleased.

Corrupting was easy, but it was for his own good.

CHAPTER 5

The Baldacci sisters lived in a luxurious chalet on the border of town. I walked there under a blazing sun in the early afternoon. They had phoned me only a few minutes before and I was told that it was an urgent matter, of utmost importance, whereby I carried with me all you need for the last rites.

The two sisters were Pina and Annamaria. The first and older of the two, was a widow. We had done the funeral for her husband just two weeks earlier. They had been married for fifty years; it is hard to find motivation to go on living alone after a life spent with a husband. Faced with certain losses all could appear empty and meaningless. Maybe it was a question of heartbreak, as they said. It was not a medical term, but summed up the situation well, the sudden lack of a partner who was now an integral part of Pina's life, being seventy years old, tired, full of aches and pains and nothing to live for. No, it was for sure Pina. Annamaria had never married. In my opinion she was a lesbian, but of those who keep it all inside a closet and do not accept what they are.

When I reached the house, it was almost two in the afternoon. It was a beautiful building made in the late nineteenth century, with a large garden all around. Some cypress trees were making shadows and were blocking the slight breeze that until then served to remove the sweat from my forehead. They were probably planted some fifty years before, when the couple had bought the house.

"Father Venanzio, please, have a seat," said Pina coming to open the door and shattering all my theories about her heartbreak, which I had developed in my mind until then.

In the living room I saw also Mrs. Gina the next-door omnipresent lady. Her role was of added sister, for long-standing friendship, counterpoint, backing vocals. The two were inseparable as Abbott and Costello, Laurel and Hardy, Vodka and Martini.

"Did something happen to your sister?" I asked looking around.

"No, Annamaria went to the grocery store. But sit down please. Would you like some coffee?"

A cold beer would have been better but I agreed. You could smell the aroma of arabica beans coming from the kitchen and the question was rhetorical, of course. I would have been given a coffee no matter what.

"What's the emergency?" I decided to ask finally, after having tasted the coffee silently.

"It's about my husband, the bastard!" said Pina bluntly. Then she got up, went over to the table, picked up a stack of letters and papers and laid it on the coffee table in front of me. If she hadn't had curlers in her hair and a flowered robe, she would have looked good in a Perry Mason movie. Here's the evidence, overwhelming.

I looked at some papers, bank statements, collection letters. Gina shook her head.

"He spent all our life savings and put a mortgage on the house," explained Pina. The outrage was slowly taking over the awareness of being in trouble. She must have been seventy years old and at that age you would not surely want to start a life from scratch.

"After all the sacrifices we made to put away some money."

Maybe on her side, certainly not the dead one, I thought. The husband had made some money when it was still possible, being a smuggler between Switzerland and Italy. Cigarettes and little else. Then he moved to Bareggio where he had lived off the interest and married Pina. They could have lived decently but then Domenico started making bad investments, chasing the dream of easy money, never real, until he lost a fortune. The wife and sister would have to live with the consequences.

"How much are the dues?" I finally had the courage to ask.

"One hundred thousand euro," said Gina. Pina had a lump in her throat and could no longer speak. She sobbed. First the loss of her husband, then the discovery of the debts. She began questioning her entire life.

"How can I help you?" I asked. It was a genuine question, perhaps she would have needed a lawyer.

"You have studied," said Gina, "we looked around, the gold is gone and even those few jewels she had. What is left is the furniture, a few paintings and library. You know, Domenico always said *invest in knowledge* and he was never wrong. At first we thought he was saying it as a joke, that studying is important. But he always bought lots of books and behold, maybe a library might want them to buy them all. Some are old, you know? Old stuff. We might not make a fortune out of it but maybe we can keep creditors at bay for a while."

They led me to the library, as if I had been an antiques dealer on a war footing. If you could not help, you had to at least spend some time listening to the miseries of others, pretending to care. That was the job.

"If you don't mind, I'd like to look around a bit," I said.

"Sure, go ahead," said Pina. "If you want another coffee ..."

"Maybe later."

It is always a wonder, with people. Domenico was a simple man and yet had a large room full of books, a real library.

I looked around. Pride and Prejudice by Jane Austen, first edition. One hundred euro. And the old man didn't even know English. A row of books nearby said *Dizionario Sacro e Profano di Pivati*, some beautiful gold rimmed leather books. I had a quick look at the first book. Published in Venice in 1746. If this was not going to bring in a few thousand euro, if sold well and through the right channels, I was a Muslim.

A Divine Comedy of the nineteenth century, several Bibles. I opened another. It said *Comparatione Torquato Tasso con Homero e Virgilio, insieme con la difesa dell'Ariosto paragonato ad Homero*. By Paolo Beni all'illustriss. & Eccenenentiss. Sig. Don Giovanni Conte di Ventimiglia, published in MDCXII, which meant 1612. A buzz distracted me from reading those ancient leaves, the air conditioning had set in motion. Only then I noticed on a shelf one of those tools that trace the temperature and humidity of the room.

Come off it, I told myself, someone is taking me for a ride. Domenico the smuggler had an ancient library that Umberto Eco would envy. I was stunned, I should have said to the old lady "Tomorrow I shall come along with a van," I'd have to load all the books and escape abroad. They would have paid for beers, joints and whores, for two or three lifetimes. And instead I sat on a black leather armchair, gazing at all that treasure. Maybe the same Domenico would sit in that armchair, maybe on a Sunday afternoon, trying to gaze at those works. If I did it right, Pina would have given a substantial contribution to the Church (or maybe I'd reap a minimum commission on the revenues by selling those books). That would kept the Bishop happy for some quarters.

All those books would need to be catalogued, if we were going for the auction option.

"LOOK BETTER," said the voice of God,

stentorian as always.

I was getting up when my gaze ran over a display case, like those used to keep cigars. I opened it and inside I found a Bible. There were white gloves at the side, so I wore them before opening the sacred old book. It was made in parchment, written in Latin and in gothic characters, with decorations and fabulous pictures.

I put it back and I headed into the living room.

"Mrs. Pina!" I called.

The two ladies came out of the kitchen with some fresh steaming coffee, on a tray. They were ambushing me at the doorway.

I asked her if I could take away two or three books to be evaluated and I received their assent. "Go ahead," she said, "where Domenico is now, he doesn't need them anymore. He spent hours in that library. I'll buy the one I read on the used stall at the Sunday's market. Those in the library I've never read. Not my thing, I like Harper Collins."

I asked for a piece of cloth, I wrapped the Bible in it and then rested it with care in my bag.

In the cabinet there were some documents, a Palaeography study of the work, which ended up also in my bag. Some bills and receipt for renting a warehouse and a key resting on it; the address for some warehouse in Pero. Who knew, I thought, maybe I could find some old contraband cigarettes; I put the receipt and the key in the inside pocket of my jacket. I took a couple more books among the ones I had examined, keeping them under my arm and exiting the building I promised the two old ladies that I was going to come back soon.

Fuck, it would take weeks just to catalogue all that stuff.

CHAPTER 6

"Where are we going?" asked Peter who had now assumed the role of leader of the group of Africans.

"I'm taking you on a field trip, I told you. And then you are going to earn a couple of hundred euro without having to carry around bags and merchandise. Don't complain." The group was not convinced but it was easy money, I promised that we'd be done in a couple of hours, and they got into the van.

We arrived at the safari park around nine in the morning. I did not expect to find many visitors, especially on a Wednesday morning and in fact there were none. The guy at the check-in didn't even make the effort to ask himself what would a priest and four black dudes do in a park thought for kids. He gave me the tickets and recommended not to exit the vehicle under any circumstances.

I found the right spot ten minutes later, twenty meters away from the guided path. The trees were right, not too thick, the grazing light was brilliant and most importantly, no one in sight.

"Come on guys, take off all your clothes and

put these on". I had given them some straw skirts I had acquired from the parish theatre. They had been used in a play a long time ago, before my time in Bareggio. They would be on the tight side because my companions in crime were big men, while the costumes were made for sure to be worn by kids. So much the better.

"Venanzio, have you lost your mind? What kind of a joke is this?" asked Peter.

I wasn't going to tell them a lie: "I need some pictures of an African tribe and I don't have the money to go to Africa myself, I thought I'd put together a photographic set."

Peter was not impressed: "What about taking some pictures off the internet? Did they seem too bad?" The others had not yet understood what I was asking them to do, so they kept waiting hoping that Peter took the right decision for everyone. Some barely spoke Italian.

"The pictures on the internet are protected by copyright."

"Are you stupid or what, Venanzio? You worry about shit like that, while you have not thought about the consequences of what you're asking us to do. No, I mean, imagine the headlines. Catholic priest caught taking pictures of half-naked guys in a children's park. First, they are going to lynch all of us and then they ship us back to Nigeria. You would go straight to jail." He was on a rampage. I would have said red-faced, if he wasn't black.

"Listen, you want to earn these few hundred? I swear we'll do it quickly." I didn't want to do a stump speech or try to convince the crowds. What I was asking them to do was stupid, but I didn't have a better idea and it seemed the right thing to do at that moment. Peter was busy in talks with his mates for a few minutes, considering the pros and cons. Eventually they decided.

"Okay, okay. But we want a hundred bucks each."

"You got it!" Bastards, they were taking advantage. "Come on, take your clothes off and wear the skirts before someone spots us. We take the pictures there," I said pointing to a sapling down about ten meters from the car.

I checked the camera and it seemed fine. I got out of the truck and opened the rear doors. I had found some short Zulu spears and faux zebra-skin shields. Peter shook his head, resigned.

"You first, Peter, after all you are the tribe leader apparently." Peter was not amused by my attempt at humour, "Sit on your skirts and watch the horizon, looking for a future for you and your family ... that's good." I took some pictures.

"Listen, give it a shrug to that big dick of yours, doesn't seem big enough in the photo."

"But we're doing a porn calendar? I knew you priests were dirty minded, but here you are passing the limit," objected the chieftain.

"No, nothing like that, the purpose is to make some parishioners horny." I had to tell them the whole story. Someone laughed at the thought of becoming the masturbation object for the local grannies. "Come on guys, show some butt. That's you, Obomo, bent over to pick something up. We are going to make Bareggio the wettest town in the hinterland. A little to the left so I can include that giraffe neck in the background. That's good."

"Mr Venanzio," said Obomo, "there's a lion."

I looked around and actually I saw the beast not far away, which was showing some interest in our charity work. I thought about a strategic retreat, imagining the headlines the next day "priest mauled by a lion while preparing to take porn pictures of black dudes in a local zoo." The Bishop would not be impressed.

"Don't worry" I said, that's a male. It's the

females, those without mane, which are dangerous. Those are just big bored pussies."

Peter kept looking behind him, like a hunted bank robber.

"Don't worry," I said, "they keep the lion well fed every single day, they can't even move so they are full and asleep. Come on, still a couple of shots and we're leaving," I encouraged them, but I myself started having some doubts. A slight breeze had arisen and who knew where it was carrying our smells.

"Hey, the lion started a trot, what are we doi ..."

"There's another one," cried Obomo, "Father Venanzio…"

I was already running towards the van and the group didn't wait too long to follow suit. Already the lions were launched in pursuit.

"Fuck! Run! They are behind me!"

"Open the door, open the door!" cried another. Luckily, I hadn't locked the van. I jumped into the passenger side, the hell I would have wasted time walking to the other side of the vehicle to go to the driver's seat. For all I knew, on the other side we could have had cheetahs, crocodiles, anacondas. My buddies did the same and they huddled eagerly against each other on the back seats.

"Close the door! Close the fucking door!"

A pair of Lions had arrived and now they were watching us, paws on the door, as they would with canned food.

"Fucking hell Venanzio, don't involve me in any more of this crap!" cried Peter.

I was laughing like mad. "What, don't you go chasing lions every weekend, in your country? Test of Manhood and stuff?"

"I grew up in England, you Christian scum. I don't know shit about lions. And don't believe that ancient roman bullshit that lions only eat Christians ..."

Maybe I did a number on this one. "Come on guys, put your clothes back on. You've earned that hundred bucks apiece."

They were too shocked to discuss or negotiate a higher price. While they dressed they kept watching their backs. We carry in our DNA certain fears. I jumped over the seats until I reached the driver's seat and put the van into motion.

We returned to Bareggio in religious (each one in its own way) silence.

CHAPTER 7

I had studied the route. Postmen ain't got shit on me! I was optimised, better than if I had a GPS. I had spent the night studying the route after buying a map of Bareggio from a newsagent. I had divided the town into sectors: the green one contained the houses and buildings where I could get more money. I would have bet on the guilt, the inhabitants of that area knew they were earning good money. I would emphasize diseases, poor nutrition, the lack of the most essential things.

The yellow zone was the most difficult, people who work very hard, with a handful of change to bestow. But for those I had my secret weapon.

The red zone was full of miserable sods and I would consider going there only if I hadn't taken enough from the first two. Blessing of cars and homes, we pray together, give me some pocket money, 'cause these Africans can eat for a week with that sort of money.

I filled the bag with printed leaflets from the website and I went on my way.

"ARE YOU ON THE RIGHT PATH?" asked God, "HAVE YOU ALREADY GIVEN THE

GOOD NEWS?"

What the fuck did he mean with the good news? God, Christ do not speak to me through riddles, tell me how it is and be done with it.

I took the phone from my jacket pocket and dialled the number of the Cernusco parish priest. Fuck, I was already sweating, who the heck had the great idea that priests should wear black robes in summer? Under the scorching sun. The Pope thought it through. All white, as Gandalf after he had plunged into the Ditch to Moria. No sweat, fresh linens.

"Hello."

"Marcello, Venanzio speaking."

"Are you all right?" asked the priest on the other side.

"Yes, look, I went a little overboard with the Bishop," I confessed.

"Don't tell me, I'm back five points on charity and this year he raised my target by 7%. I'm going to steal to make a difference. Or worse, I might have to work. The excuse is always that targets are imposed from above, there is also the crisis of values, the Church must survive. I never saw a bonus once in a while." Then a pause. "You went overboard in what way?"

I told him about the App and the idea I had

presented to the Bishop.

"For Christ's sake, Venanzio! What the fuck do we know about computers? Though the indulgences part seemed to me a good idea."

"Do you still have that contact at HP? Can we blackmail him somehow?" We were in a bind and something had to be done.

"He has a mistress. A chick that would awake Lazarus without the need for a miracle. And his wife is a little bitch, but she is the one that has the money. She wouldn't like to know what her husband does in the evening instead of meeting with American colleagues."

"Look, set up a meeting. You do the good priest I do the bad priest. We are going to convince him one way or another; I've already made a list of things we need," I said.

"I will let you know later in the week." So saying, he hung up. There were still two quarters to the end of the fiscal year. With a good result I would have taken the Bishop off my back for the rest of the year.

Marcello was a good guy who didn't make a fuss and especially he had a clear view of how things should be done. I would have voted for his election as Pope, had I been a cardinal. He was that sort of guy who could bring fresh ideas on how to rejuvenate the Church. On second thoughts, maybe I would have not voted for him, they would have killed him in his sleep like they did with the other one. A drop of poison in his coffee and get the fuck out. Whomever was too innovative was not well seen in certain environments.

At last, I reached Fiammetta's villa, my first visit for the day. She was in her early fifties and she had never married, thanks to a mother with an iron fist. She owned a medical analysis laboratory, which she ran personally. A wealthy circle of friends, including a soccer player, now retired, and several friends who were spending money on plastic surgery and jewellery as if it were the last chance to look decent in this shred of life. For some of them it was.

Fiammetta had split the house into apartments, often rented to foreign students or young professionals who did not want to pay the hefty fees in Milan. For sure she had some money set aside.

She came to open the door in a petticoat and when she saw me, she ran back to get a robe. I wished I was a plumber or the postman. Not that she could hide those two big tits anyway. They were equipped with a life of their own, they were dancing all over the place, they came out of the tiny bra at every movement and poor Fiammetta tried each time to sort them, trying to put them back in place. Not succeeding.

"Please come in, Father Venanzio. What an unexpected visit." She turned on herself and led the way to the living room. A smell of braised steak hovered around the corridor and made me want to drag this out longer, at least until lunchtime. The room had a couch and paintings on the walls, dark furniture certainly bought by her mother and never changed. Out of respect, because Fiammetta was a little stingy, probably because every time she looked at a shop, the severe mother was judging her, from up there. Surely with a face full of disapproval. Perhaps the only step out from the dictates of her mother was her short hair, almost a crew cut, platinum blonde. They looked right on her, made her look younger, almost sexy, although anyone with common sense would never reach such heights: they would be bewildered by looking at her breasts.

I sat down on the couch next to her. "We are doing charitable work to help these children in Africa." I opened the bag and took handouts from the website, the one with the kids. I told her of the pains and sufferings that the poor children had to undergo every day. Kilometres to fetch drinking water, contaminated, brown in colour due to dirt and impurities inhabiting those wells. I pushed as much as I could, telling of swollen bellies like balloons, sad eyes they could not cry anymore due to lack of drinkable water, an uncertain future made of miseries. For those who would survive, in fact most died. Yellow fever, malaria, diarrhoea, malnutrition. Fiammetta listened and didn't beat a hair, the only concern was not to burn the sauce that was boiling in the kitchen. I saw that sometimes she turned her head in that direction, not paying too much attention to what I was saying. I was going to say that the stew she was preparing would had been enough to feed those kids for weeks but that would have been too pathetic. So, instead, I talked about the parents and relatives of those kids. Meaning Peter and the others I took photos of.

"See?" I said, handing over the pages of the shadow site, the one never published. "The parents need to get their food from the bush, risking their lives every day to put something into the bowls of those poor creatures."

Fiammetta was flabbergasted. "But they are practically naked!"

"Well, Fiammetta, they aren't like us. They are still stuck to basic needs, food, water, sex. You know, that is fertile ground for Islam, if we don't put some effort to help them."

I made up a typical day for these poor individuals, walking through long hours to obtain food, the danger of the lions (that was true, I'd experienced it first hand), and of course the only consolation in a life of misery was sex. These poor souls didn't know better. Every day, after they returned from a long hunting trip, they had nothing to do but to cut loose with their wives. "Think about the poor women, Fiammetta. They spend the day caring for the poor children, to weave wicker and then in the evening these thugs force them to have sex without having a second thought about it. They do not even have a book to read before going to bed in the evening, the Bible for example. Instead, these brutes are back from the hunt, all sweaty, they lift their women and carry them into their hut. I would not go into details but you know that the average penis in Europe measures approximately 13 centimetres? These guys will have thirteen centimetres at rest, when excited, I wonder to what extent they go." I made a gesture with my hands to give her the idea of the length of an aroused dick.

Fiammetta held her legs tight.

I continued, "They throw their women to the ground (with all those shiny muscles you can see in those pictures, it won't take any effort) and jump on them like animals. They penetrate the poor wives in all possible ways, they are savages, Fiammetta, they want to hear the wives cry and moan when they do certain things. They don't know civilisation as we do. Imagine a whole night passed in the clutches of these individuals, naked, full of desire and lust, wanting to be sexually satisfied. No matter how much a woman says no to those attentions, they take them every single night. And this because they still do not know the ways of the Lord like we do."

Fiammetta was red in the face and feeling hot. She untied the robe and the glimpse of those big tits almost made me lose my train of thought. I continued to describe the tribal practices, of how women could be sold in exchange for a sheep or a cow. How they were penetrated at every occasion: they were pagans, the hunting tribal rites obviously included the sacrifice of some poor virgin, group sex, rape. All hunters in the village would have violated the designated virgin. I stopped at nothing, I plucked stories out of thin air and had it not been for Fiammetta's mother, the spirit still hovering in those places, the woman would have masturbated in front of me. She winked at her fingers, she held them in her lap while listening to my fable, red in the face, well aware that she wanted to place them elsewhere.

When I finished my story I told her of the website where we were raising funds to help these poor things. "Obviously if you want to make an offer, we also take cheques. We were also thinking of bringing some tribal chief here, to let them understand that there is another way to live their life. God's way." I aimed my finger at Peter's photo, pointing at his big, black cock in plain view, "We need to let them learn not only about our religion but also about our culture and values."

"Of course, of course. A cheque." Fiammetta looked around, got up and went to open a drawer in a cabinet next to the window.

"Obviously I wish they met some of our parishioners to understand our way of life."

Fiammetta jotted down a number.

"I'll talk with my friends," she said, finally, handing me the cheque which I put in my pocket without looking at it. Never judge other people's generosity.

There was always a moment of embarrassment when money changed hands, it was inevitable. Hard earned saving given away in an instant and then the thoughts: have I done the right thing, have I given enough. Or too much. Over the years I had seen that too many times, and try to avoid that silence prolonged more than the necessary was now an art that I had aged.

"How are things going, Fiammetta? Are you still renting the apartments to young professionals?"

"Of course. Next week comes a consultant from Rome. By chance, he was looking for a hotel and since they are all full because of the Expo, the person at the concierge, a close friend, sent my name. The company he works for did not think for a moment about the price I asked. Compared to hotel prices it is a nice saving, you know? He came to see the apartment the day before yesterday. Quite a serious, strapping young man in a suit and tie. A professional."

"I'm glad," I said. And I meant it.

"Before him there was an artist. A Canadian girl who studied painting for a year at Brera. She was a little wild, you know? She found a boyfriend from Sicily. One day I was looking out of the window and I see him coming in a hurry, throw his scooter on the ground and running up the stairs. After two minutes I hear screams, "ahhhh!" and then "ahhhhh!" and I thought, oh my God he's killing her."

"Do not tell me, those Sicilians are dangerous."

"Of course, I was scared. I started listening to the door to figure out what was the bone of contention, and those screams continued. Then I realized they were doing something else. Oh my God, Father Venanzio, I've been thinking about it all day, I even wet my panties. Those Sicilians are known to be on the wild side when it is a matter of sex, but I wouldn't have ever imagined as fiery as that."

"You are right, Fiammetta, but they are young, sooner or later those youths put their head right," I said. At that point I already pocketed the cheque, and then I liked to be the one telling the stories, not listen to them. For that there was the confessional.

"What smells so good?" I asked her to change the subject.

"I'm making beef stew in red wine, by the way, I have to go and add some water otherwise it sticks to the pot and then it tastes burnt."

I followed her as she headed toward the kitchen. Her butt was not a large one, I would have said "the right size", as I liked them. Fiammetta was not overweight, you would have thought so by just looking at her from the front, those huge breasts did take blunders. I was getting hard by seeing her in her dressing gown cooking, and then I was always left in doubt of those big tits: would they have been hard or soft to the touch?

Fiammetta added water in dribs and drabs, she tasted, stirred, in short, she was wasting time.

"May I taste?" I asked approaching her from behind. I put my body against her, pushing with the belly to her back. My erection was halfway through, but my dick was well placed between her thighs. I reached out with a hand from behind and reached for the wooden spoon, taking it to my mouth. If it had not been for the hostess' breasts to make my dick stand, that stew would have sufficed.

"Perhaps a tad bit of salt," I said putting the spoon back into the pot. Fiammetta made no objections. She moved leaving the butt propped up against my willy, she stretched in order not to lose that contact that, sure enough, kept alive the excitement of a few minutes before. In the meanwhile, I had moved my hands on her hips, like if I wanted to avoid stumbling. And I'd grinded against her. I wanted to hold her breasts, but still hadn't come the right moment.

"What do you say now?" she passed the spoon back. The sauce was perfect.

"Much better," I replied. I held her firm against me, in case the mother's ghost appeared suddenly and took her down to Earth. I enjoyed seeing her committed to doing things on hand, check the potatoes, stir the sauce; Fiammetta would do anything not to depart from my hard member pushing against her, she even invented non-existent culinary activities.

The flesh is weak, I always said that, so I lifted up her robe from behind. She had nice white lacy panties, a shame that no one else had bothered to look at them first. I caressed her hips, my fingers crept under her panties, which I found wet, needless to say. I slide them down and opened the zipper of my pants. I didn't remove them, it isn't polite having a priest butt naked in the house; who knows what the neighbours would have thought about that. I pulled my dick out, I pushed

Fiammetta a little forward and my penis went smoothly in without a hitch. They all lost their virginity in random circumstances, one over a fence and one for a shot too strong took on the swing. Fiammetta groaned. I pushed strongly from behind, I didn't want her to regret one night as a prisoner of Peter's tribe. I grabbed those two big tits from behind, which were decently hard. A doubt resolved. I felt her nipples harden under my fingertips. She kept cooking and I kept pumping from behind like a maniac. She came soon enough, with a nice moan and a sigh, I followed her to wheel shortly after. I came inside her, I already knew she was on the pill. She had confessed it to me weeks before. Because they settled the cycle, she knew that doing certain things were a sin. I pulled a sheet of paper towel and I cleaned myself. This time no sacred Shroud, no crying Jesus Christ, only sperm on a napkin. I breathed a sigh of relief.

"Do you want to stop for lunch?" she asked, always stirring the pot roast. The best fucks were those where the parishioners kept going on in their business, as if nothing had happened.

I not only would stop, I'd even considered being adopted by her, but instead I said, "No, thank you, it is best if I continue my quest. Those poor creatures await."

I got out of the house and my legs had the jitters, as if I had climbed the Colle Brianza cycling.

I couldn't have managed to finish the round that I had set, while in the head I reverberated *Hit the road, Jack*. This time the Ray Charles version. There was nothing to add, he was right, I had to soldier on.

CHAPTER 8

It was a dark and stormy night.

Well, not really; it was definitely night but mostly there was an insistent drizzle of the kind that washed the bones more than a downpour.

"AND THEN YOU TELL ME WHAT SHALL I DO!" I cried hurling the Corona bottle against the wall.

"YOU CAN'T ALWAYS DO WHAT YOU WANT, VENANZIO. THERE ARE RULES." boomed the voice of God.

"And who is going to stop me? Are you going to send me the locusts, get me red water out from the tap?" How did he not understand? He was supposed to be omnipresent and mighty, why for once wouldn't he give me an answer rather than leave me to my fate.

"THAT IS PRECISELY THE POINT," said God, reading one of my thoughts.

Yes, that old story. We talked about it at length and eventually he also probably decided I was a pain in the arse. He didn't tell me openly, but I could tell by his tone.

I sat in the armchair and I opened a cold

beer. I drank a sip and then a second. I half expected that he would comment, saying that drinking wasn't good for me, that I was ruining my health, and instead he stood silent.

There are those who in life seek solace in religion and who, living by religion, don't know what to do with it. For me it wasn't much different from working in a factory or an office. I had to still obey and comply with the rules that someone smarter than me had imposed.

In the dark, in that ghostly silence, a light settled on the shelf across the room. It was like a theatre spotlight pointed on a stage. It was illuminating a baseball signed by Joe DiMaggio. It was not original, of course, the signature. I made it myself, but I kept in in there out of curiosity. Sometimes a little too curious parishioner went snooping around in my office, and as soon as he identified the signature, he was left speechless. They would stand there frustrated because they didn't dare ask: I was too young to have received it directly from the hands of the player. Maybe it belonged to my father, but they wouldn't enquire. Fathers die and no one wants to be so insensitive. At most they said "Oh, Joe DiMaggio..." and I would say "Yes" and nothing else. The fact that baseball was so out of place caused them to think. The lack of response was working as a worm in their head and I was enjoying watching those scenes.

I got up and went to the cabinet. Under the baseball there was a wooden club. I tried once to convince the boys in the oratory to play baseball. Only five of them agreed, but after five minutes they had already lost interest. The stories about the Red Sox and the Cubs faded like mist in the sun.

What was left was the bat that, rather than the ball, was what I needed most. I took it in my hands, I twirled it a few times by mimicking an unlikely home run. It was heavy, exactly what I needed.

"VENANZIO, DON'T DO ANYTHING STUPID," said God.

I wasn't going to and I wouldn't have done, of that I was sure. I was fully aware of my actions. I put some beers in the bag, the baseball bat under my arm, and before leaving I grabbed a dark woollen balaclava, never used. It would not serve to keep me warm.

My beaten-up car awaited me.

I arrived at Father Zambrini's house, I parked and watched the road. You could see the rain by looking at the streetlights, a myriad of small needles that fell silent. No one in sight, it was late and people were already glued to the telly, watching quizzes where alleged graduates couldn't answer elementary questions, or to be befuddled by strips of populism, packaged as absolute truths, big brothers which resembled more and more demented cousins. In short, the field was free.

I headed over to the door and knocked on it. Father Zambrini did not ask who it was, *knock and it shall be opened*, except that instead of facing a pilgrim, a hiker lost, he stood before a big man dressed in black and with a ski mask descended over his face. He didn't have time to open his mouth because he got a baseball bat shot to the stomach. He bent in two, making a noise like a vacuum cleaner. I caught him in the solar plexus, he would not cry. A shot from below in the face made him collapse on the floor. I entered the house, I dragged him into the hallway, holding him by the foot and then closed the door behind me. As our neighbour we had the House of our Lord, there wasn't a phone to call the police in the church; it would take a computerized little miracle.

I gave another whack to Father Zambrini who, somehow, managed to raise an arm to protect himself. Not a smart move because I felt a crack of broken bones and a short gasp. He was still trying to gather his breath after the blow to the stomach. I looked at him. He was bleeding from the nose and the mouth, his eyes were pleading like those of an ox in a slaughterhouse. He wondered who, how, why, for sure.

I hit him again and then again. I kept striking him as if I was on autopilot, I felt that noise of the meat mallet until it became a plop, and moans and then silence. I had beaten him badly, of that there was little doubt. The parquet was all a bloodstain.

"WHAT DO YOU SAY ABOUT THIS?" I shouted.

Silence.

"Come on come on, let's do one little miracle for once. Otherwise, they are just words!"

Silence.

"If you're not going to respond, at least send your son. Let him show up for once and knock it off. Come down here for a party, *in the presence of God and of Christ Jesus, who will judge the living and the dead, and in view of His appearing and His kingdom*, I have a couple of things to tell you about that."

Silence.

It wasn't that bad, being in silence. At least I

didn't have to put up with all that shit that He was saying, every hour.

"Well, I'm going to fuck off then. You take care of this one. You do the miracle of saving him, he's not dead yet, you know?"

Silence.

I looked around a bit, I opened a drawer without knowing why. I didn't want to rob him, of that I was certain. Jesus Christ! I had forgotten the beers in the car. I would have peed on him and instead I jumped over, being careful not to step on the blood. I finished drinking the beers in the car, then I turned on the engine and drove home. Half tipsy.

I slept like a baby that night.

CHAPTER 9

Peter arrived around seven PM. Punctual as Immanuel Kant, but it could not be otherwise with the dishes the *perpetua* prepared.

He sat in front of me.

"Do you want a beer?" I asked.

"Wine, please. Today I'm in Omar Khayyam's mode," he ruled collapsing on the opposite chair. He had dropped the big bag containing all the fake items on the floor. A dull thud of fabric, artificial leather on the wooden floor.

"My Lips the secret Well of Life to learn:
And Lip to Lip it murmur'd - "While you live
Drink! - for once dead you never shall return," I recited from memory.

"That's right. Poet in the year 1000, forced into a nursing home and rehabilitation, if he had lived today," he said.

"With compulsory attendance to every bloody Alcoholics Anonymous meetings," I added. We laughed toasting with the only treatment available to bear with life. Wine.

"What's cooking" asked Peter.

"Our *perpetua* has done her best to boil for hours an oxtail with celery, carrots and other spicy secrets. Then she forgot, she went out for errands and when she returned the poor meat was in tatters. Luckily, I added water in the meanwhile, not knowing what else to do, otherwise we'd have boiled coal for dinner. The poor thing was desperate, but I saved her from self-flagellation, suggesting to make a ragu out of it," I explained.

"Pasta, finally," he replied, "since I got here I kept eating roasts and stews."

"The *perpetua* was horrified by the idea," I continued, "but then she came to her senses." I went into the kitchen to toss pasta into the boiling water and set the timer for eleven minutes exactly. A digital timer not like that crap they had put on the probe to Mars, the Schiaparelli comet lander, who had turned off the engines ahead of time and crashed.

"I have a couple of chores for you, Peter, nothing challenging but you could earn some extra money without having to carry around that duffel bag," I ventured.

"Fuck off, Venanzio, I've had enough of your ideas, find someone else," said Peter bluntly.

"Ah, but there's no danger here, it's a matter of cataloguing old books for an elderly in need. The salary would be minimum wage, so you get used to being an EU citizen, but I apply the German tariff. Eight and a half euro per hour. Overtime allowed."

"And the other job?" asked my guest.

I was saved by the bell, or better by the timer in the kitchen; the second task would require much more effort and persuasion on my part.

I drained the pasta, then poured it into the pan where the Oxtail sauce was waiting and a divine scent arose. Fuming vapours of pure delight. Those aromas would have resurrected the dead, *Lazarus come forth, as the perpetua made the sauce.* They didn't put that part in the Gospel, those Council of Nicaea scumbags, they were worse than the censorship in the seventies.

We ate in religious silence. To pass the wine there were gestures, at most a grunt, not wasting time on unnecessary words. As if we were still living in caves (and if there had been such nectar at that time). We had a second helping of pasta and satiated, we settled down on the armchairs.

"So, about this job?" asked Peter. It was amazing how decent people always sought honest work, even when they were living in complete illegality. He wouldn't have had a pension, nor have insurance coverage, or a disability pension if a tome had fallen on one of his feet, and yet ...

Yet a half service, temporary job in a library appeared better than walking around selling fake bags. Nobody would see it, but Peter had dignity, although sometimes I made him put it aside. He was one of us even if, because of some bureaucratic problems, the British had ruled otherwise. And so were many others, those who arrived on the sly on barges from the most remote places. Most sought just an opportunity; it was enough for them to dream of a life that equals everyone else in this country, even if we kept complaining about what we had. They would have wanted more only once they filled their belly and satisfied the basic needs. In the end we were all from the losing side, us and them; we were the same ones that they cheated, every time, with the promise of some stability.

"The job is simple: it is to catalogue all the books of a private library." I explained how he was supposed to open them one by one, scribble down the title, author, date of release and conditions on a notebook and nothing more.

"I have been to a library once," said Peter

sarcastically, "I'm amazed, people do really read all those books? And here I thought it was a special stock of toilet paper."

I thought about some book published recently, signed by some homegrown celebrities, and I couldn't disagree completely. "You need the appropriate clothing, though. You must not go there in flip flops and with your shirt greased with sauce," I said looking at him from head to toe, "here I need your Oxford experience."

"Obviously, Venanzio. You know I still have some fresh tailored suits from Bond Street, can you believe it? I have a custom made closet full of that stuff. I don't wear them when I sell the fake bags because the tie tightens the neck and gives me a headache, otherwise ..."

"Ahaha. Come on, we are going to sort out your wardrobe," I said getting up. Peter drank the last sip of wine that still awaited him in the glass and followed me.

My clothes wouldn't have suited him; holy shit, Peter was bigger than Kunta Kinte, but luckily the parishioners were generous. I had set aside the best clothes, thinking of reselling them on Ebay in case of a rainy day, and this was without a doubt a rainy day, but I could sacrifice some clothes for once. It was for a good purpose and I reckoned that Mrs Pina would be generous. A dark, grey Armani, XXL, was the first natural choice. I also had some nice silk shirts, set aside in the closet.

"By any chance, do these clothes belong to some dead people?" asked Peter.

"Why, are you afraid that the spirit of the deceased may be pulling your feet during the night while you are sleep? I thought you were a Muslim, not an animist," I snapped back.

"Asshole! No, they stink of corpse."

"But no, that's the mothballs. Just hang them outside in the fresh air for a day and the smell goes away. And then the smell gives you the academic appearance, always locked at home studying ancient texts, trust me."

He didn't trust me.

He tried a three-piece suit and he looked just as if he came out from Oxford that very day. A tie by Jean Paul Gaultier completed the outfit. Red and blue, with religious motifs, a crown of thorns, the word "amor". A little vibrant but elegant, there was no doubt I was proud of the result. I also had a brown leather bag, used but in good condition, and here was Dr. Oguntoye, fresh off a Ph.d. from Oxford at your service.

"When they're dirty bring them here and the

perpetua will wash them," I said putting a handful of shirts in the bag. The last topic were the shoes. The ones I had in his size were Pollini, like hell I would let them go. They would fetch at least one hundred euro on eBay, they were almost new. Peter looked in the mirror, turning in on himself a few times. He had sad eyes, thinking that if things had been different perhaps he could dress in Armani every single day, instead of selling handbags and watches to passers-by. I had to kill that thought in his mind before it was too late: never ever let your mind wander on certain concepts. Soon afterwards comes the melancholy, you call into question your life, and then comes the depression. No, I needed a gung-ho Peter, enthusiastic and awake, not a depressed immigrant.

"So, you show up here tomorrow morning and we go together to the house of the Baldacci's ladies."

A nod of assent, but nothing more. He still had in his eyes that self-image of himself in England; he had gone from brilliant student with a future to being a poor guy in a matter of weeks, they are so efficient the English, God curse them. Then he added, "These clothes. I can't bring them back in that rat hole where I live. They are going to steal them in no time."

Ouch!

"Let's go in the living room and I'll tell you about the second job. That should solve the dilemma." I paused for a moment in the kitchen and I opened a bottle of *Amarone della Valpolicella*, which I poured in a crystal decanter, another donation of the parishioners to the needy. That wine had to breathe and it was just what I needed to convince Peter. Sitting on two leather chairs, facing each other, we looked like two honest citizens ready to talk business, sipping wine and laying the groundwork for a prosperous future.

I told him what I had in mind and, instead of going berserk at what I was proposing, he laughed out loud. It was like thunder, a liberating sound. It was the knowledge that comes with disillusionment, that nothing is easy in this world and no matter what we tell ourselves, if things go just right, it is only for luck or intrigue.

"We start tomorrow morning," I concluded. Peter wore again his rags, reluctantly, and off he went into the night.

There was another issue that needed to be resolved.

I took my personal address book, and I searched for the number, it was not the first time that I had called him.

One ring, two rings and then three.

"Hello?" said a sleepy voice on the other end of the phone.

"Good evening, Commissioner, this is Father Venanzio."

"What the fuck did you do this time?" he paused, "Jesus Christ, do you know what time it is?"

I knew it, it was two o'clock in the morning and I was half drunk, due to having finished that bottle of *Amarone*. "Don't mention the Lord's name in vain, Commissioner," I said.

"I name the fucking names that I want! Then again, what have you done this time?"

He was not in a good mood, of that I was certain. I turned on the light on the desk and I thought for a while about how to ask the question.

"You have certainly heard about that atrocious beating against Father Zambrini, I guess," I asked tentatively.

A pause.

"Did you receive any threats?" he asked suddenly.

"Who me? No, not at all. I was wondering

how the investigations were proceeding that's all. A crime so heinous..." My palms were sweating all of a sudden. The *Amarone* was a strong wine."

"They are not going, simple as that. We have nothing, we can't explain this aggression, there is no reason, no motivation. No one has claimed it, it doesn't look like a theft ... Father Venanzio, why are you asking me these questions at two in the morning?" The voice was now firm, the voice of a seasoned copper.

"No, I was wondering if you had not had time to dig into the depths..." It was not a good night. Commissioner Toscani always spoke without mincing words and came straight to the point.

"Venanzio, if you have something to say, come to the police station," he said, cutting the chase, "no, tomorrow you come to the police station no matter what, and you tell me what you know, and no bullshit, are we clear?"

We understood each other; I would have rather avoided a face-to-face conversation with the copper but to certain orders it was better to obey. "I'll be coming to your office in the early afternoon," I added.

"And bring a lawyer, you never know." He hung up the receiver and for a couple of minutes I stood there, in the shadows, trying to figure out if he had made a cop joke or if he really recommended to seek legal help.

No, he had said they were groping in the dark.

In the silence of the night, I put down the receiver. From the window came the filtered light of streetlamps and the full moon, which accentuated the shadows of the furniture in the study. Maybe I had got myself into trouble.

CHAPTER 10

Peter arrived punctually at nine in the morning like a good schoolboy; he changed clothes in the sacristy and in suit and tie he looked just like a scholar. He was only missing the finishing touch, a pair of eyeglasses, with neutral lenses, to give him the appearance of a researcher.

"So, what do you think?" I asked when the work was completed.

"That I'm living a shitty life, that's what I think. By this time, I could have had a Ph.D. and have a serious job instead of selling Chinese bags and fake watches. If my mom finds out how I make my living, she would have a heart attack." His face was serious, tough, of those who had suffered an injustice and have no way to redeem themselves. Judging is easy. I thought about how many parishioners, without realising it, were one step away from living as Peter. They had a job, a family, a home, but many were just a couple of wages away from ruin. The bank didn't like waiting, if you missed a couple of mortgage payments, if the head of the household had lost his job, things wouldn't have turned out differently from what was happening to this poor guy. We forget that we are slaves, that they keep us by the balls all the time. Sometimes it is convenient as well, we don't worry about it, we keep going, living in the illusion of really having a future, something to rely on. They are all lies.

"Don't be negative, you look like a model, you'll make a great first impression," I said. Words lost in the wind, but that seemed to cheer him up, in that dark corner before the church. I had to take him out before he started to think too much. Thinking hurts, makes us contemplate about strange ideas, makes us realise who we really are. Better to be busy, with anything, a scam, a canard, work, it doesn't matter.

Just off the church someone called me "Father Venanzio!" For Christ's sake, in this fucking village, parishioners ambushed you and I had no time to waste.

"Good morning," I said. I remembered the face but not the occasion, or the name. We shook hands and the stranger started talking, "Thank you for the kind words you said at the funeral, I was really impressed, you know? Even my dad, who now observes us from up there, would have been pleased." He oozed gratitude and faith. In that moment, I remembered. I offered a mass a few days earlier for a Mr. Bellani, recently departed. The wife of the guy in front of me had also tried to barter on the price for the mass, "Couldn't you do eighty euro? You know, with all the bills for flowers and the coffin." She tried her luck; everybody tries to pull a trick and avoid paying and that just pissed me off big time: all that money spent on the dead and nothing spent for the living ones.

"So, you didn't understand a damn thing about what I said!" I added whilst I kept walking. Peter was following me like a pet, moving his gaze from me to my interlocutor, not knowing whether to intervene or not.

"What do you mean?"

"I mean that your father is NOT watching from up there. He is in a shallow grave in the churchyard with worms feasting on him. He is eating carrots from the root side. He's dead, buried, that's it!"

"But ... How dare you ..." he stammered.

I gave him no time to retort, "when you are dead, you are dead. Do you want to understand once and for all that the deceased don't go on a cloud to heaven? Where the fuck were you during Ash Wednesday, on vacation in Ibiza? *Memento homo quia pulvis es et in pulverem reverteris*, By the sweat of your brow you will eat your bread, until you return to the ground— because out of it were you taken. For dust you are, and to dust you shall return! Crystal clear, your father is in the quagmire of the cemetery with moles, worms, bacteria and beetles. Pigeons fertilizing the grass above him. I would say may God have him in His glory, but I highly doubt it. Didn't you read Saint Paul? He talked about the resurrection of the flesh. Not now, when Jesus Christ finally decides to pay us a visit, until then we are dust. He didn't mention anything about little souls with wings flying to paradise..." Peter placed a hand on my arm to make me stop.

The amazement was rapidly leaving my interlocutor, while anger grew quickly in him, nudging as a late commuter during rush hour. "This is blasphemy! You will get in trouble ..."

I left him there on the road yelling expletives toward me while I signalled to Peter to get into the car. I would have left with a wheelie if I hadn't a clunker of a car.

I drove slowly, I could not do otherwise, with my gaze lost on the road in front of me, the traffic was light but cars were starting to get in line to get to the highway. Fortunately, the Baldacci ladies weren't living too far away.

"Fuck, Venanzio, you could have taken it easier..." Peter finally said.

"Sometimes I lose my patience, I can't help much with that. Look, let me do the talking when we get there."

"Yes, bwana, at your orders, bwana."

That made me laugh. We arrived at the house shortly after, and I rang the doorbell. Mrs Pina came to open the door without the escort of the almost inevitable Mrs Gina, she greeted me, took one look at my partner and she let us in.

In the living room awaiting us was who I knew to be her niece, Philippa. She was in a wheelchair and she put down the book she was reading as soon as we entered, by coming out to greet us.

"This is Dr. Oguntoye," I said, "he's studied at Oxford and he's an expert in old books. He will catalogue your library to give us some indication of the actual value of the works." I said. Peter made a half bow and sat up in a chair, I chose the couch, next to Philippa. It was summer and she wore a pair of shorts the like of Daisy Duke; a beautiful woman of twenty-five, with copper red hair that covered her shoulders. What a waste to see her in a wheelchair.

"Philippa, we meet at last, I have understood you are now a writer in the making." I've never grabbed the legs of a paraplegic before, and out of curiosity I put a hand on her knee.

"Ah!" a static charge gave both a shock. Fucking clothes from the flea market, made of nylon and polyester. I promised to myself to ransack as soon as possible Mrs Pina's husband's clothes. I would have asked for a donation or some other dances.

"Yes, I am an author of dystopian," she said, "I have already published three novels."

"A great satisfaction, right, Mrs. Pina?" I asked.

"I understand a little about those things, I like Harper Collins," she said, and that killed the talk on literature before we even started it.

"Well then, I'm going to show the library to Dr. Oguntoye," I said.

"Shall I make a coffee?" asked Mrs Pina.

"Thank you," said Peter, "if you don't mind, I would prefer tea." Faux pas, Mrs Pina had asked me and in certain environments the hierarchies needed to be observed.

"He's English, you know, they prefer tea," I tried to explain. "Doctor why don't you follow me to the library?"

We took our leave and once in the library I closed the door behind me. "Ok, these are the books to be catalogued. Don't leave out anything, if you find also a copy of Tex Willer, catalogue it, name of the work, author, year of publication, the books condition."

"Who the hell is Tex Willer?" asked Peter.

"Local celebrity in form of cartoons admired by kids. You write everything in the notepad I gave you and when you're finished let's see what we have."

"Yes bwana."

"And if you find something relevant mark it with an asterisk."

"At your orders, master."

"Ok, I'll stop being a pain in the arse, message received. Here are twenty euro, there is a restaurant at the end of the road. I'll pick you up around five PM."

I left him struggling with the goods and I got out of the library. Mrs Pina was waiting for me at the gate.

"Father Venanzio, the coffee is ready," and then whispering, "but is it safe? You know, he's a negro ..."

"Mrs. Pina, he might be a negro, but he studied at Oxford; if you want, I'll send the busboy from the bar to do the job, who is white!" I said.

"Heavens no, I didn't mean that..." I'd embarrassed her. Some things made me really angry.

"See, Mrs Pina. Let him work and take to him all the tea he might want. It depends on him if we find some work of value, so please, keep him happy." I greeted Philippa and I went outside.

I lit a cigarette, I took a big breath and the good Lord was back talking to me, "YOU ARE SUCH A DICKHEAD!"

"Tell me something I don't know already."

"WE WILL DO GREAT THINGS TOGETHER."

Yes, how to bring God's Word to prisoners, for example. The Commissioner was waiting for me.

CHAPTER 11

The Rho police station had recently been moved to what used to be the building of the *Liceo Rebora*, one of the Rho high schools. The school was not so great before and despite the renovations it still looked crap. The entrance was a grey cube that brought sadness just to watch it. A row of non-EU citizens were waiting their turn for a visa and they were lined up outside, under the sun; they were accustomed to do so in their own country, or so it seemed. A separate door was left open for us humans. It was a matter of waiting our turn anyway and in front of me there was a fat man with a greasy shirt; he held a towel on his head, in an attempt to staunch a wound. What the fuck he was doing at the police station instead of the hospital was a mystery that the law enforcement agency would fix soon. A well-dressed lady was busy explaining out loud her own business, the police officer was taking notes but it was evident he had had enough of the lady also. Apparently, the police had messed up with her daughter's passport. No, she couldn't come personally, she was a Manager in a major company, with a row of executive meetings in Los Angeles and Dallas. Finding that passport would surely save the world from an economic collapse, the officer went out of nodding and taking more notes, then got up to go to another room.

The lady hadn't finished yet. Now she stared around in search of looks of approval, she was proud she was giving a hard time to those clueless chaps at the police station. I avoided crossing my eyes with her and the cougar began to puff.

The officer returned with a colleague who knew more and then looked in my direction. The fat man next to me was complaining but what he said was nonsense, at least in the current Italian language, so I jumped the queue and I stepped forward. Best to talk to a cop than stay there one minute longer, with the smell of pee that hit your nostrils as if it was ammonia.

"Tell me," said the copper. No hello, no smiles.

"I'm here to see Commissioner Toscani, he is waiting for me."

"Third door on the right down the hall," said the cop with a raised voice. One of the immigrants had enough of the fucking wait and was arguing heatedly with the guy before him in the line. Ah, the privileges of the clergy. A white collar so the police didn't even asked for an ID.

"Come in," said the Commissioner. He hadn't even glanced at me, busy as he was reading a document in a folder. Bloody hell, in the computer age here they were still working with paper placed in yellow folders. Fluttering pages, coffee-stained, that told a one-way story, the police version. No room for conjectures or justification on those pages, just facts.

Behind the Commissioner, a big man in his fifties, a little overweight and with a beard like Fernando Rey, you could see the portrait of the former President of the Republic, half covered by the Tricolour Flag. The furniture was functional, it gave the idea that everything had a reason for being there, from the shelves with the folders to the coffee table and the large wooden desk. No frills, paintings or objects that could make people feel at ease. The only concession, the photos of his wife and two daughters, placed right next to the computer screen, strictly turned off.

The leather chair on which I sat made a fart noise, which the commissioner pretended not to notice. I was wondering if I could get away with a real one.

"What can you tell me about what happened to Father Zambrini?" he asked without looking up from the papers. He had a strong voice, a baritone voice, with a slight accent from Piedmont.

"A very regrettable tragedy indeed. Of course, if not even a priest can feel safe..."

"Father Venanzio, if someone threatened you, you have to tell me in no uncertain terms, especially when it comes to any Islamic Group. Not that there are many in this country but you never know."

He was shooting in the dark, which made me relax. The Sun was filtering through the window behind him and launched reflections on the metal edge of the computer. I squeezed my eyes for a moment.

"No, no threats. I was wondering if there were any developments in the investigation, that's all."

"Venanzio," this time he looked me straight in the eyes, "don't take me for a ride. You called me in the middle of the night, if you want to know the latest news go buy a newspaper or else you can get out of my way. Or say what you have to say. And if you learned something by way of a confession, at least give me some clue."

That was the problem, trying to spit it out without getting incriminated.

"May I ask you a question?" I asked.

"Maybe I wasn't clear, I'm asking the questions here, and you answer them," he said annoyed.

"In my humble opinion, if there is a lack of clues, perhaps it would be worthwhile to expand the investigation. If nothing comes out, maybe not on Islamic side, perhaps delving into Zambrini's past, even the most recent one might unearth clues that could be of use."

"Thanks for trying to explain to me my job, Father Brown, aren't you watching too much television lately? What clues are we talking about?"

"We priests we often find ourselves in a position of trust, but we are still human beings with our flaws. If someone had been wronged and had been unable to obtain justice..."

The Commissioner stood up abruptly and went to the window. He remained silent with a blank stare (or maybe he was looking at the long queue for the visas, I could not decide) and then he smoothed his beard, trying to find the right words. Then he turned his face towards me, stared at me straight in the eye and said "Jesus Christ, the guy is in a coma, Father Venanzio. What the hell happened?"

"Is he bad?"

"There is a good chance he will spend the rest of his life in a vegetative state, drooling on his shirt."

"Good. I mean, I'm glad that the situation is not life threatening." I didn't realize though if that "what the hell happened" was directed at me or was a generic question, but with that cop I should tread carefully, or sooner or later he would have guessed my involvement in the matter. "I came to know that he took advantage of a few kids and, you know, there are limits which, if passed, could lead someone to take revenge."

"How sure are you about what you are saying? It is a heavy accusation," said the copper, still standing in front of the window.

"Pretty sure, people do not confess certain things to a priest just for fun."

Toscani opened the window, pulled out a cigarette from his jacket and lit it. He was the law in that very moment, he couldn't care less of the prohibitions. I would have smoked one myself, fuck I would have smoked a whole packet due to the fear I had of the commissioner, but I just didn't want to push my luck and ask for one. Luckily, he saw my ravenous eye and he offered me one, quietly.

He gave me a lighter and I took a breath.

"But don't you have some sort of law that prohibits you priests revealing what was said in a confession?"

"Ah yes, the sacred and inviolable seal of the confessional. The fact is however that the confession was made to me by his partner in crime."

Toscani bent his head forward by surprise, he looked at me through his glasses and immediately I could hear the copper wheels grinding in his head.

"I ask again, are you sure? Because we are going to create a stink, here."

"I would say yes. And I don't think the two are security wizards, Zambrini had a computer ..."

"Maybe you should let us do our job," he interrupted me, when in fact he should have asked what I knew about that computer. I saw it that night and I hadn't resisted, taking a peek at what it contained. Knowing that Father Zambrini was out of circulation had made me feel better, after what I had seen on that computer. "There's more?" asked the copper.

"There would be a little thing that I would like to bring to your attention," I said shyly after taking another breath from the cigarette. I tried to blow smoke towards the window, without succeeding. Toscani had smoked his in an instant, long and powerful pulls, he was a chain smoker in need of nicotine. He motioned me to continue and so I told him what I had in mind.

The thing made him smile but eventually nodded in assent. "Bugger off, Venanzio," he said. I stood up and walked toward the door.

"Sooner or later we will catch the guy who sent Zambrini to the hospital," he said.

"What do you mean?"

"Probably they used a baseball bat. You know, it is not enough just to clean it, traces of blood soaks into the wood and you can analyse them even years apart. It is enough having a suspicion to issue a search warrant. If he was smart, he threw the bat in the river Ticino or burned it. But perpetrators are idiots, they never do it."

He was right, it was still in the trunk of my car. Wise words that I would follow to the letter.

CHAPTER 12

There was little else to do that afternoon, other than wait till five PM and go to collect Peter. The oratory was deserted, the church as well, apart from the usual pair of little old ladies who were sitting about halfway up in the church. When you did not have air conditioning at home, the church was one of the few complimentary places where people could receive some relief from the summer heat.

I wanted to send a message to Simonetta but at that hour she was in the office. Then she would go home and cook dinner for her daughter. No chance of a shag until the weekend. What a rip off.

I went back to my office and I opened a cold beer. The next day I would have to meet Father Marcello and his trusted programmer so I started writing some notes about what I wanted in that App.

A calendar with pre-set timer for the Vespers, morning prayers, festivities. List of rolling prayers, to read in case anyone had forgotten. Latest news from the Holy See, online confession chat.

Where was that coming from? No, nobody with a bit of sense would put their sin in writing. *Scripta manent.* Too many issues with security and privacy. Booking a confessional appointment was a far better idea: find the nearest church via geo location and schedule an appointment.

The donations section, indulgences, etc. We accept PayPal. Something was missing. The sin.

A notification that in fifteen minutes would have been the time to recite the Vespers wouldn't work. Email and text messages were coming in every hour of the day on mobile phones. No, we wanted something different. The notification would come the next day, "Yesterday you forgot the evening prayers," or, "It's 124 days since you haven't helped the Church with a donation" attached photos of miserable, hungry children, the ISIS was gaining proselytes. And a list of sins, random: "Did you lie to your wife today?" "Did you remember to go to church last Sunday?", "Did you follow the dictates of Christ within the last 24 hours?" As a result, the *donate* button would appear, nay, the *ask forgiveness* button, that invariably led to the donations page.

I worked on it for a few more hours until it

was time to go and fetch my faithful Oxfordian. With five beers in me, I drove very carefully.

Peter was still in the library filling annotation sheets, aided by Filippa who had taken an interest in the matter. Mrs Gina was not in sight. Weird, I could have sworn they would be watching "the negro" at every step, fearful that he would pocket the silverware at the first opportunity. And instead, nothing. Maybe there was a future for humanity.

I greeted Filippa and her beautiful legs, Peter did the same and we set off to my car.

"How was your first day?" I asked.

"That guy collected weird books. I found some first editions, literature of the nineteenth century, but most are ancient texts that I don't know. I climbed on mirrors trying to see them at ease. The granddaughter came to see how things were going and asked me a mountain of questions?"

"Did you bullshit her? What did you say?"

"That it would take time, better not to overreach on certain things. And then we started to talk about other stuff. About Oxford, the period I spent in England and things like that," said Peter, staring at the horizon as we headed towards our next destination. "You know she is a writer?" he asked at one point.

She was one of many. Now it was enough to write a few pages, post it on Amazon and boom! a writer was born. I even thought of getting myself involved in that trade, with all the free time I had, but what could I have written about?

"Her next book will be a best-seller, *The Virgin and the librarian.*"

"Venanzio, has anyone ever told you you're an asshole?"

Many. Peter was mad as hell, you could see it. I would have liked to put a microphone in that library and know what the hell they had been talking about all day, but then it was none of my business. I was just hoping he didn't take too seriously that little job I had entrusted to him. It was easy to dream about normality under certain circumstances. Only to face the hard reality later.

I wanted to explain, and instead I only said a "Sorry" that Peter seemed to accept.

I drove in silence until we arrived almost at our next destination. I turned into a dirt road between fields with rows of trees on either side, on the edge of the village, and turned off the car.

"Come on, get changed," I said handing him back the skirt of straw that he had used a few days earlier. He said nothing, he seemed troubled, oddly, since when I had mentioned the matter he had just laughed out loud. Eventually he obeyed.

The naked body was covered with a blanket, just in case a cop car had passed by and they took a peek into my car.

We reached Fiammetta's house a few minutes later. *Knock and it will be opened to you.*

"This is the chieftain Oguntoye," I said presenting the proud warrior behind me, armed with a spear and a shield made of zebra skins.

"Yes, Yes, come in," said Fiammetta, looking around from the threshold of the house. Who knew what the neighbours would think, seeing a priest and an African chieftain on her doorstep.

She led the way and we followed in the living room, Peter was behind me with a stern and noble look.

"I pray take a seat," said Fiammetta pointing with her hand toward the couch. Peter remained standing next to me.

"GUANDA KOBALI HAKUMI," he said in a stentorian and authoritarian voice.

"Botanga bowindi hakumi, Makali gatala," I explained my best tone of haughtiness.

"What did he say?" asked Fiammetta intrigued.

"Nothing, it's their greeting when meeting foreign leaders. I told him that we are among friends and that he can sit. Peter squatted on his haunches. He was without underpants and he was showing his big salami dangling between his thighs.

"As I said by telephone, Fiammetta, we will find an accommodation for our guest soon. Thank you for the hospitality you showed us. We want to make sure that the chieftain sees how much Christian charity we have. This is the first time he has left his village and therefore he is wary, but I'm sure that you will introduce him properly to the Gospel and to the words of Christ. If not in words, at least by gestures, you know, a good gesture is worth more than a thousand words.

"GOBANDI KAWALA ISSUMI ATAKA. GOBANDI ARIKUM ASAWILI," said the Chief.

Fiammetta turned to me and asked, "He would not be dangerous, would he?"

"Well Fiammetta, he is a tribal chief. He says that this is the time for the lion hunt in his country. You know, a little danger is always there, they are savages living a tough life and they are accustomed to violence. Barbaric acts have been perpetrated in his region, women kidnapped and put into slavery, violence, rape, tortures. But Chief Oguntoye was very courteous with us, he understands that we want to help his village, he also knows that we Westerners do good. I'm counting on you to show him the way of the Lord. However, if at any time you feel in danger, don't hesitate to call me."

"Sure, sure. Thank you for trusting me, Father Venanzio."

"But of course, it is me who has to thank you. I have to run; I leave you with Chief Oguntoye. And please, Christian charity. Oh, no spirits or alcohol, they always use them before going into battle and they become violent, but maybe with just a glass of wine you should be safe enough. And no overly processed foods, they don't understand them. I'm not saying to give him raw meat, although I have heard that in some cases in those villages they have eaten the still-beating heart of their enemies. Well, maybe a steak, rare, roast chicken and chips, simple things for simple minds."

Fiammetta continued to move her gaze between me and Peter; she didn't look at him directly, for reverence or perhaps to focus better on his dangling dick. I suggested Peter to splash some oil on his muscles to make them shiny, but Peter did not want to know. Too bad for him.

I made the universal gesture of who decided to bugger off, that is, I stood up. One last warning to the chieftain: "Akali matanga."

I received a return salute and Fiammetta walked me to the door.

It was going to be a long night.

CHAPTER 13

I went to collect Peter the next morning. I had brought his suit, a white shirt and a red tie freshly ironed by the *perpetua*, belonged undoubtedly to someone who had died.

"So, what have you learned from our Christian society?" I asked as soon as he was in the car. He tried to squeeze in his trousers, with many difficulties.

"Oh, several little things," he chuckled.

"Don't keep me in suspense," I insisted.

"Well, first of all, Catholics are clean. Fiammetta explained to me diligently how I should wash my hands before dinner. Unfortunately, I tried to drink water from the bidet and that must have upset her a good deal, because she started to say "no, no, no," a lot. And then she tried to explain to me what the darn thing was needed for."

"In words? "I asked curiously.

"Words and gestures, which I ignored bluntly. I don't think she could make a living as a Marcel Marceau lookalike. She rubbed her hands and then pointed at my jewels. The poor thing, she was so frustrated; then she thought of explaining the use of the bidet in Italian, but more loudly, as if the volume would have any effect on understanding. To my AKABALA KOTANGA of frustration (She must not be very skilled in Klingon's language) she snorted. She made me sit on the bidet and then, reluctantly, showed me what to do."

"Did she wash your willy?" I asked. Not that I was astonished, just curious.

"Apparently you Christians pray during ablutions. She covered her hands in soap and then she started washing my cock. Each wipe was accompanied by a "Oh my God" or "God forgive me". I had never read this subtlety before. Well, the fact is that all that rubbing of my knob, sparkled another set of prayers, especially when I had the mother of all erections. The poor thing was red faced and embarrassed but I could tell she wanted to explain properly how to wash my dick. It seemed she was polishing silverware," laughed Peter.

"Hygiene is an important thing in Italy, not like in your country where you cover yourselves with mud to keep away the flies."

"That is what elephants do, you moron. Well, I said, after the ablutions she took charge of drying me. The penis is a delicate area, never let it be that somewhere is not completely dry. Morals, with all those attentions she almost made me come. And then came time for dinner. The problem was that with all the attention, I was hard and my dick was sticking up out of the skirt. A spear ready for combat. The poor thing was pretending to ignore it, but every three seconds she gave a peek, she blushed and then returned to cook."

"Maybe she was anticipating a plate of stewed sausages, who knows?" I said.

"An attention to sausages worthy of the best chef," said Peter. "However, I am guilty of having been distracted in the kitchen."

"What did you do?" I asked amazed.

"Nothing, really. With all those culinary odours around I was curious and so I started to peek at what she was cooking. The fact was that, being still excited about all that washing my penis had suffered, I had it straight as a nail and every time I looked at what she was cooking my *membrum virile* crashed into her butt. Apparently, you Catholics also pray in the kitchen. I realise this is a very Catholic country, but I never imagined how much. The poor thing was stiff as much as my penis and she threw a few little screams at each contact. So, I decided to finally put my dick between her legs."

"Don't tell me that you made her commit a sin!" I said with my best outraged face. In fact, I'd walked that road just a few days before, nothing would astonish me.

"No, not at all. Just a rub, some little cavorting. An anthropological experiment to see her reaction. To my disappointment I must say she took it well. She continued to cook as if nothing had happened; apart from a bit of sweat on her forehead and reddened cheeks."

"What did she prepare you for dinner, then?" I asked curiously.

"Steak and chips. Calling it steak would be an insult, it was four fingers tall. Of course, I ate it with my bare hands, to her immediate horror. She got up abruptly, as if I had just committed a sacrilege. She moved her chair next to mine and started off with a new set of instructions. Always in Italian of course. This time I pretended to understand, to her great joy. I might be a savage, but I have some brains; Fiammetta realised I wasn't hopeless after all. Encouragement is everything."

"Oh," I said as I continued to drive, "then it was a quiet evening after all, apart from the ablutions, right?"

"I would say yes. At least until I raped her."

I locked up the break and Peter, with no

seatbelt, went slamming against the dashboard. The car behind began tooting for my sudden manoeuvre. Followed by swearing and rude gestures until the driver noticed that I was a priest. He gave me one last fuck off, respectfully though, before the car moved away.

"WHAT?" I asked.

"Your fault, Venanzio. You left a savage with a white woman, what did you expect to happen? The fact is that after dinner she went to get comfortable wearing a dressing gown that would make a dead man hard and took me into the living room to watch television. Attenborough's documentaries, and Rai 5. I don't know maybe she wanted to make me feel at home, the fact is that at one point there were two lions shagging and I kind of was in the mood. I wanted to ask her to explain to me again how the bidet worked, but I was under instructions not to speak in Italian under any circumstance. We were sitting on the couch and then I took her hand and I put it on my willy. So, just to see what would happen. She retracted it saying a lot of no, that it was a sin and stuff like that. I might have been a guest, but behaving whilst she was half showing those big breasts was not so easy. Then I went on top of her, as you would expect from any self-respecting chieftain, who take what they want."

"Jesus Christ," I swore.

"And anyway, apparently, it's not polite to rape a white woman on the couch. In fact, as soon as she got free she took me into the bedroom. The cougar knackered me, it seemed I had stuck my dick in a milking machine, I'll get a prize for sperm donor of the year."

"Peter ..."

"Yes?"

"Fuck off!"

Peter was silent for a moment, probably without experiencing any repentance for his own actions and then he asked, "Can I borrow your computer?"

"To do what?"

"I have to write an anthropology essay about the hidden desires of the white women."

"Peter, fuck you!"

"I take that as a no."

I could lend it to him in the end; it was in my office collecting dust and I wouldn't have used it for all the gold in the world. I thought of giving it to George as a price for his website creation. I knew that wasn't the real reason, but sometimes lying to myself was the only way to feel safe.

Then Peter said "Anyway, you heard Fiammetta this morning; she said to take me back tonight, so maybe you could give me the mitigating circumstances."

I burst out laughing. In fact, I had not thought that Peter could get to that point with Fiammetta. My error, the woman might have been in her early fifties but she kept herself in very good shape. I had a boner by just thinking about her, and then all the coaxing over sin. They were an invitation to shag her. The only issue was about the donations. I thought about using Peter to attract more faithful, put him on display in front of the beguines and let them wrest on who would make the best donation to the parish. If Fiammetta was not stupid, she would keep the thing about Peter under wraps, hosted him in a warm bed as long as possible and then ... once I removed her toy, she would not say a word to anybody.

I should have thought it over.

"Ok, I'll lend you the computer. So you can use it also for the cataloguing job. Jesus Christ, I didn't think you could take her to bed on the first night."

"Venanzio, for once I followed the directions of your Gospel, quenching the thirsty, and Fiammetta must have spent the last twenty years in a desert from what I saw. I had to fuck her in positions that aren't even in the Kama Sutra, and licks this side, and penetrates this other. Take her from behind, above and below. She would be a good director of porn movies, if you ask me. Shit, when I fell asleep you could see the crack of dawn out of the window."

"Too much detail. Shake a leg and get changed, you cannot go to the Baldacci ladies with the skirt of straw. We need your best Oxford attire, and we're almost there. I will bring the computer this afternoon."

"Aye, Aye, Captain."

After I had left Peter to the Baldacci, I drove in a hurry towards Milan. Maybe I should have changed career, maybe I should have worked as a salesman, at least they took commissions for their bullshit. I was earning one thousand two hundred euro per month. Apart from those few pennies I stole from the charity jar, those small donations coming from time to time, such as Fiammetta. There was an advantage though. Nobody was asking for a receipt and no one went to ask the Bishop if he had received the money. Unless they were important sums.

I parked next to the main train station and the gypsy on duty came to beg some money. Novice, we had two thousand years of experience in helping us taking money from others. The trick of the bundle in the shape of a baby was old, it would not work on me. "Go fuck yourself," I said.

"I wish you to stay healthy," she said back.

"And I hope you return to your country poorer than when you came here. Get the hell out of my way before I call the police."

Various insults followed, curses on her side, only partly in Italian, but they would not set, I was a servant of the Lord after all.

The interior of the central station was worse than I remembered, it seemed a concentration camp for blacks and Moroccans. Some asking for money, others trying to steal it. Nothing new from that point of view, we were doing the same, it was the way we did it that was the only difference, not the substance. I had pity for them, sorry guys we arrived first, if you want to steal, take your number and line up in the queue.

The usual tourists were hurrying up the escalators with giant, unlikely suitcases, a couple of cops were throwing a kick at a tramp that was sleeping on a marble bench. The station was a mess but they had to also keep a minimum of appearance.

Father Marcello was waiting for me at the bar upstairs. Next to him, a guy in his forties wearing a suit, named Riccardo. After the introductions I explained to him what I wanted in the App, I had even made some drawings of the screens, the complete list of functions, what was a paid function and what was not.

"Have you ever thought of becoming a programmer analyst?" asked Riccardo. "You did a great job, usually when they give me specs they are half baked, foggy."

"No, never. Cut to the chase, how much would this App cost me?" I said tucking away the sheets of paper. It seemed a clandestine meeting between Russian and American spies, with the only difference that we weren't in Vienna or Prague.

"A rough guess would be thirty thousand euro. It is not an easy job, if you want to get it right."

"Would ten thousand do and I'm keeping the source code? In return, we give you absolution for all your sins, past and to come for the next 20 years," I suggested.

"Fifteen thousand, I have a mortgage to

pay." "Look Riccardo, this is a job you do on the sly. I'm sure in your employment contract you have some intellectual property clause. Ten thousand is a good price, and I know that in the evening you'd still write programs anyway instead of numb yourself in front of the telly. This money is bread that you take away from children in need, families in poverty that the Church is helping ..."

"Okay, okay, I get it. Twelve thousand and you got a deal," he said reaching over the table.

"Wait, hold your horses. Delivery times?" I asked while moving the beer away. Spilling beer on the floor brought bad luck during a business meeting. It brought bad luck anyway.

"Would three weeks do?" Richard knew what he was doing. We signed the agreement with a handshake as you do between gentleman, and our programmer bogged off. We would hear from him when we had to test the App.

"Fuck, Venanzio. Twelve thousand euro. You threw me in the shit, what the hell are we going to say to the Bishop?" said Father Marcello. The awareness of being exposed too much was making him freak out. He wasn't a bad guy, maybe just a little fearful.

At that time, I received a message on my

mobile. "Speak of the devil, and the Bishop sends me a message. There are divine powers at work, Marcello. You let me work and you'll see that everything will fit into place."

"What does he want?" he asked craning his neck and trying to peek at the screen.

"He wants to see me immediately; it doesn't say anything else. Look, I'll keep you updated on this." I stood up from my chair and I shook his hand. Marcello remained seated in his place. He wasn't completely wrong, if we messed up they would send the both of us to Riccione as punishment.

CHAPTER 14

Immediately is a flexible concept. I had to wait nearly an hour before being admitted into the Bishop's presence. The heavy oaken door opened and, to my surprise, I saw Commissioner Toscani exiting the room.

He noticed me and he nodded. He wore a light grey suit, white shirt, blue cop tie. Maybe that was the way they chose commissioners, unable to sweat even in a day hotter than hell.

"Commissioner, good evening."

"Don Venanzio."

"How are the investigations going?" I asked.

"They proceed. But go to the Bishop who is eager to meet you," and off he went, walking as if he was in a military parade. Stiff as a piece of steel, grim-faced.

The Bishop was immersed in reading lists and statements. If they were the same as the previous time, it was not given to know. I walked over to the desk and waited patiently.

"What the hell have you done, Venanzio?" he asked suddenly, without looking up. His skeletal hand was pointing to one of the chairs facing the desk. I sat down.

Difficult to answer at that juncture. The

thing that worried me most was the visit by Commissioner Toscani. He didn't lose time.

"What do you mean?" I said with a voice as innocent as the situation could afford.

"I have received a complaint. This guy, Augusto Trombetta, phoned us repeatedly until he was able to talk to me. He said you have insulted the memory of his father and he is accusing you of blasphemy."

"Ah, that," he was referring to the guy who had approached me after the funeral of his father. "I have not insulted anyone, I only made him aware that his father is not in the Kingdom of Heaven. Or at least, not yet. St. Paul clearly speaks of the resurrection of the bodies, *Jesus will come to Earth to judge the living and the dead*, meaning all the *men*, past, present and future. And unless there's been a zombie apocalypse in the last ten minutes ..."

The Bishop stood up from his chair, "Don't come here and quote the Scriptures to me, Venanzio! I know them by heart and thank God I can still interpret them. With these things you need to use some tact, damn it. You can't go around making certain statements. People talk, it is a damage to our image. With statements of that kind people might stop donating their money to the Church. Have you ever wondered what would happen if instead of having the hundred percent turnout in church there was only half of the people?"

I never asked myself.

"Look, you see? You don't think about those things. You don't see the big picture. Those are funds that allow us to work, to keep the structure of the Church intact." He began to walk silently back and forth as if he were looking for a solution. He kept his hands behind his back. Then he sat down, he probably had already reached the maximum number of steps allowed for one day. "But that's not why I made you come here."

A most memorable silence was never uttered.

"The man you saw going out is a commissioner. You must have heard or read about what happened to Father Zambrini."

I certainly did, and I had followed the commissioner's advice to get rid the baseball bat. I nodded an "of course."

"That attack is not just the result of some crackpot; the commissioner is investigating a network of paedophiles among our ranks. Zambrini is in the hospital with a guard at his side and today they have also arrested Father Rossetti."

Father Rossetti was another priest, the one that came to me to confess his sins. Toscani was working hard and fast, there was no denying it.

"There is nothing to investigate on me," I said. I wanted to add "on that front" after all I had some skeletons in my closet too, but not in that sector. Who knew why the Bishop used the surname for some priests, such as Father Zambrini, and for others only the name. I was always Father Venanzio. Maybe he didn't even know my surname.

"Yes, I know, I know. Unfortunately, I have to ask you to take charge of the second parish in Bareggio, the one managed by Father Rossetti. In these dark times of crisis we can't be seen weak."

"Sometimes it would help if we were not seen as paedophiles in the first place," I said half aloud.

"What did you say? I didn't catch that. Do you mind repeating?" asked the Bishop.

"No, I said, sure, I will obey and I will take charge of the parish. Trust me, Bishop."

The Bishop, Father Filiberto, nodded and relaxed on the leather chair. He ran his hands over his eyes as someone who didn't sleep at night or who must try to capture an elusive thought. He seemed to have aged ten years. I decided to try my luck.

"Bishop, I know that you are an expert in sacred literature," I said.

"Oh, I wouldn't say an expert, just a mere admirer of the work done to celebrate the glory of our Lord," said disdaining, "but tell me."

I told him of the Baldacci lady and how I had come across that ancient Bible. "Next to the Bible there was a palaeographic analysis that attributes the work to the school of Johannes Grusch in Paris. You should see that bible, written in two columns per page, parchment, it still has great colours although there are signs of wear on the edge of some pages."

"You said Johannes Grusch?" asked the Bishop with renewed interest. "Please, describe it!"

I gave the best representation possible, trying not to forget details. Every now and then the Bishop asked for more details about calligraphy, images and so on. I could barely describe what I had seen, I knew I wasn't doing justice to that job. The Bishop stood up and went to get several books from the library. He showed me different styles, pictures of parchments that appeared to me all the same (yet they weren't). I did again refer to that palaeographic study I had read, but I could see that what I was telling him wasn't enough to satisfy his curiosity.

"Father Venanzio, do you understand? An incredible discovery, if it were really a bible from the Parisian School of Johannes Grusch. Do you think it would be possible to see it in person?"

"I guess so," I said, "the Baldacci lady is trying to save her house and get some money. They are in debt and I really think they would be willing to sell it."

"Don't tell her this, but a Bible of that type could cost up to two hundred and fifty thousand euro."

Bloody blimey, that would have solved the old lady's issue and some more. Or mine if I decided to do an elopement with the money.

The Bishop was as excited as a kid. The concerns of the previous hour had disappeared to make way for this new discovery. A mere admirer. Hell, I knew full well that he was a top- notch collector. And then he had family money, nobility titles. He would certainly try to screw the Baldacci lady into a crappy deal, maybe asking even for a donation. I would have to instruct them adequately before they would meet this shark.

"Bishop, before I go ..."

"Certainly Venanzio, tell me."

"Do you remember that I had mentioned to you about that App? The one with the prayers on the phone and so on? I met an analyst today and an indicative estimate is around twenty thousand euro. The application may be delivered complete in about three weeks. Think, they wanted thirty thousand euro but I bartered downwards, I know these are luxuries we can't afford."

But Father Filiberto was lost in dreams of ancient Bibles. He mumbled a "no problem, you can get the funds from my secretary," and he dismissed me.

The day couldn't have gone better.

CHAPTER 15

"What's for dinner?" asked Peter heading directly toward a bottle of *Sassicaia* which I held for a special occasion.

"Baked pigeon in red wine sauce with mashed *scorzobianca*, or salsifis as would say the French, fondant potatoes, glazed carrots and peas. The pigeon was killed in full accordance to the Halal dictates, with a Kalashnikov."

The bastard uncorked the bottle without even asking. At least he had prepared two glasses.

"Go easy with that, cowboy," I said, "later on I have to take you back to Fiammetta."

Peter was troubled, different from the usual. He sat in front of me, twirled a few times the red nectar into the glass but not able to bring himself to gobble it. Something was wrong.

"Ok, spit it out!"

He scratched his head looking for the right words, staring off into space or maybe staring at a particularly interesting tile on the floor. "The fact is that for once I feel normal. Don't get me wrong Venanzio, I'm well aware that what I'm doing is all bullshit, it is a short-term thing, but finding myself in the middle of that library, discussing literature with Filippa, is making me think about all the things that I have been robbed of. A decent life, a job."

"Filippa? Ah we are at first names now. Is it not that maybe all this melancholy is basically a sentimental issue? Until recently you were selling fake watches and you never batted an eyelid about the shitty job you were doing, and today we are talking about Filippa. What future do you have, assuming you two have one? You are an illegal immigrant and she is in a wheelchair. You are not even considering taking her back to your hut village in Nigeria. You ran from that place as if the devil himself was chasing you. And as soon as you try to make this interest to a most serious thing, you hit another brick wall: a visa, the racism, the lack of a proper job." I wasn't helping, I knew, but in certain situations it was necessary to face the hard reality, or it inevitably would bring more trouble. And then there was the story about Fiammetta and other beguines. I needed a Peter healthy in his mind and in shape, at least until I could scrape together a sufficient number of cheques.

"No doubt that when you want, Venanzio, you could be a real asshole."

You haven't seen anything yet, I thought. "By the way, here's the laptop and please, use it just for working purposes, no porn on the internet. You know how we Catholics are sensitive with these sort of issues."

"Venanzio, if your line of work wasn't being a full-time bastard you could be a comedian," laughed Peter highlighting a row of white, perfect teeth. "Come on, light a fire under those pigeons, I am hungrier than a wolf on a salad diet. The Baldacci might be good Catholics but when it comes to feeding the poor, they leave something to be desired. If it wasn't for the sandwich that Filippa brought me..." Peter realized too late the misstep, but for once I decided to let it run.

I went into the kitchen. The bulk of the work was already done by the *perpetua*, God bless that lady.

"So, the plan for tomorrow is simple," I said tasting the sauce, "you work as usual at the Baldacci's house and list all the books in an Excel sheet. I don't need a definitive list but I'd have to get in touch with an expert who could give us a good evaluation, though partial. One of these nights we shall go to Fiammetta for the second part of the show."

Peter poured another large glass of *Sassicaia*.

Who said that the bloody Muslims would not touch any alcohol?

"What would it be?"

"I was thinking of doing an auction. A dozen ladies who will compete to take care of the good chieftain. Minimum donation from everyone and who offers more brings you home for the night. You know, have the ability to educate you on the verb and on our ways."

"Fiammetta style?"

"Not necessarily, some of them might also be shy, maybe they will limit to inspecting you and make you an ablution, who knows."

"What is in it for me?" asked Peter. Who knows, maybe he was pulling back because of that interest for Filippa. I had to nip it in the bud any possible doubt he had, considering I had just been funded by the Bishop.

"Apart from the privilege of shagging white ladies? Three hundred euro in cash. Brand new bills ready for a long trip to Africa via Western Union."

"Deal done."

I told Peter about my meeting with the Bishop, omitting the details about the commissioner. If that was the price for a single book in that library, the entire collection would probably be worth a fortune.

"Please tell me you are not going to steal from the old ladies?" asked Peter. I was offended by that statement; how could he think that I would have made a mockery of someone else's trust.

"Seventh, do not steal, says our Lord."

"Yeah, the ten commandments, those are good. Your God was supposed to be a first-rate narcissist. Most of the commandments are about him. He could have added a nice don't rape, don't violate the laws of the State, remember to pay taxes, and instead nothing."

"Finally, an interesting question, apart from that it's your God also. The differences come later, with the Prophet. So let's see, at number one we have: *I am the Lord your God, who brought you out of the land of Egypt, out of the house of bondage. You shall have no other gods before Me.* Our God wants exclusivity, on that no objection," I said. I was just hoping not to hear his voice after a few seconds.

"I got another one," I said, "since we're on the subject of narcissism: *'You shall not make for yourself an idol in the form of anything in the heavens above, on the earth below, or in the waters beneath. You shall not bow down to them or worship them; for I, the LORD your God, am a jealous God, visiting the iniquity of the fathers on their children to the third and fourth generations of those who hate Me, but showing loving devotion to a thousand generations of those who love Me and keep My commandments*' What do you think, Peter?"

"That you have screwed up big time, especially with making images of what there is in heaven and on Earth. But judging from the next sentence and that outrageous impunity of yours, your great, great grandfather must have been a God-fearing man. Or more likely among your ancestors there must have been a monkey that he liked. Otherwise, I cannot explain why He didn't blast you out of this world with a well-aimed lightning bolt."

"Hey, wait a minute," I retorted, "a thousand generations, if we make an average of thirty years per generation, the thousandth generation was thirty thousand years ago. Let's say a religious Neanderthal. That sounds better."

"Suit yourself, Venanzio, I still think it was a monkey." Peter stood up and headed for the wine shelf, God save us, I thought. And in fact he took a *Bolgheri superiore Ornellaia*, which I saved for a long time. Damn alcoholic cannibal, vampire of wines. When would he stop ransacking my bottles?

"Then there is, *You shall not take the name of the Lord your God in vain*," he hinted from the cupboard, corkscrew in hand ready to kill the cork that had rested in that bottle for almost ten years. "That must have been mistranslated. Had to be Ivan. You shall not take the name of the Lord: Ivan. Your God is Russian, what about that? This makes a lot more sense, I would say. Or maybe there really was an Ivan who kept repeating the name of God in vain and God got fed up, hence the commandment."

"It could have been. The Bible is full of mistranslations. Or the New Testament, like the story of the camel passing through the eye of a needle. The Aramaic word for rope, kamilon, was almost identical to the Greek word for camel, kamelon. Hey, maybe they mistranslated also that story of yours about the seventy-two virgins. Maybe they meant seventy-two bottles of extra virgin oil. How about that?" After a bottle of wine and a second coming in I had no more certainties. The pigeon was ready so I began to serve. Lumps of peas and carrots, potatoes all around and the pigeon, split into two over the whole thing. Sure, I should perhaps have worked harder on my presentation, but fuck, I was a priest, not as if I was on MasterChef. Saint

Torode pray for us and forgive us.

"Hurry up Peter, it's ready," I said setting the plates on the table. "We forgot *Remember the Sabbath day*. There must have been a mix-up at some point because later it became Sunday. Well, maybe we wanted to make sure to not get confused with the Jews. No, pour that wine properly. Fill the fucking glass."

The glasses met doing a resounding "cling", probably to the health of both.

"Oh Venanzio, aside from the three or four commandments that followed, that maybe are the only reasonable ones, let's not forget the other commandments *'You shall not covet your neighbour's house. You shall not covet your neighbour's wife, or his manservant or maidservant, or his ox or donkey, or anything that belongs to your neighbour.'*"

This posed an interesting question. Nobody would go to prohibit senseless practices; the question of the slaves was particularly intriguing. "What do I think? To certain practices it is hard to say no. Strange that they put the donkeys on the same level as slaves and wives. I wonder how our ancestors spent their time, before the advent of television."

"Speak for your ancestors. Hey, this pigeon is excellent. Tell me, is this *perpetua* shaggable?

Because with these delicacies that she prepares..."

"She is married to God, and even if she wasn't I doubt that she might be interested in you. Generational gap, she must be in her eighties."

We continued to eat in religious silence (each one in his own way).

CHAPTER 16

George was walking impatiently throughout the sacristy, a lost soul looking for solace. "Father Venanzio! Father Venanzio!"

"I'm in the office," I shouted. I watched him from behind the glass window going back and forth, searching in the confessionals. It was a lacklustre morning and I had to prepare the sermon for the Sunday mass. One also for the other parish. For sure the faithful had read the news about Father Rossetti's arrest and I should give them a strong message. Instead all I could do was to roll cigarettes one after another. No additives, this time. I had a pile of them right in front of me that would have sufficed for an entire week.

The fact was, what to say to the faithful? I would have to tell them that one who spends his life to pray to an invisible being and makes a vow of chastity might not have all the wheels in place in his brain. No, I mean, after 2,000 years they were supposed to figure out that something was wrong in this institution. Even leaving aside the issue of virginity and the miracles, it was enough to look at the opulence of some churches to get upset. Whenever I walked in San Fedele in Milan I was cramping. How much had it cost building that bloody Church? And the Dome? With all that money spent they could the solved the housing crisis for a generation.

And the *Creed*. Who had ever really spent time to read it or trying to understand the words that were repeated as a chant every Sunday? The Apostles Creed spoke of resurrection of the flesh, *'the forgiveness of sins, the resurrection of the body, and the life everlasting.'* it seemed clear enough to me. Maybe the problem was in the Catechism. That was one of the crucial points, give them a nice explanation, the *interpretation* of the Church, and let them understand what they want to understand, and away you go with the chants.

Dear parishioners, has there never been any doubt in your mind when the priest, in confession asks you "are you touching yourself" and then wants to hear the details? Is there really the need to know the extent of sin and repentance, or more likely the priest is looking for details to then go and have a wank in peace a few minutes later? Or maybe someone masturbated directly in the confessional, I wouldn't be surprised. The seminars were juvenile rape factories, and you leave your children in the hands of these people? Send them to the park to play football, they might not be raised Catholic, but really, is it a drama? Better having an agnostic son than a raped one but Catholic. Wake up, get out of the Church and for the sake of your children, don't trust anyone. Especially a priest.

Ah, if the confession was done both ways. If before going to confess your sins you could hear of the demons that dwelled in the confessors. Then you would just run like hell, you would take in your hand pitchforks and rifles and you would start chasing the monster.

What was I supposed to tell them, that he was a lost sheep? I didn't feel in the mood to take the piss out of the parishioner that way.

"Father Venanzio, they're waiting for you for the training."

Jesus Christ, the rugby. I had accepted the post in Bareggio for that reason, and now I was neglecting the rugby team. It would have been a miracle if we had finished in the middle of the league. I had a lot of things on my plate, but it was not fair to overlook the rugby guys. Enough with the excuses.

"Make your way George, this week we play against the Lomazzo, right?"

"Yes."

Lomazzo was going to be a tricky game but nothing compared to Desio, who was our *bete noire*. The year before I had pulled up to the boys before the game. We went by train to Lomazzo and once at the station had done the voice of the stationmaster: "Who does not get out of the train down here, Lomazzo!" which sounded very much similar to the Italian *lo ammazzo*, I'll kill him. Unleashing the hilarity of those present. They were young, they were having fun with little things, but by that time the joke appealed to them and at every foul in the game they kept repeating "Now Lomazzo". The opponents did not understand.

"Listen, I had a look at that website which you made me prepare, you know, the one regarding the aid for Africa," said George.

I'd forgotten about that, I was so taken by other matters that I hadn't checked the online part. I wouldn't have done it anyway; I hadn't opened a computer for centuries. "Is everything okay?"

"Just fine, there are almost 15,000 euro in donations. Real money. But are we sure this is a legitimate thing?"

Bloody Mary, that was good news indeed. For once maybe things were going smoothly, like hell that the Bishop would put his grubby hands on the loot. That would be my retirement fund if things were going for the worst.

"Don't worry, George, it's all kosher. Indeed, maybe one of these days we work on the PageRank and SEO of the website, just to make it a little more popular."

"PageRanks are calculated according to external links, how do we influence them?" asked George.

"There are ways. You'll see."

"Father Venanzio, you said you don't use the computer yet it almost seems to me you know more than I do in the computer field."

The guy was sharp and suspicious. Good for him, a fair amount of disbelief in this world doesn't hurt. Or maybe he clearly knew that the site was nothing more than a nice scam and he kept quiet. The majority of charitable associations in the United States were real criminal organisations, if you asked me. They were paying themselves golden salaries and were passing crumbs to the needy. I would buy a new computer for George, corruption was better than threats. I would have said I was buying it for myself, asked his advice for specifications and then I would've subcontracted it to him.

The guys were lined up on the field and ready to harm. They were almost all coming from the technical school in town, one was a bricklayer and he also did a couple more jobs that I didn't remember but they were the kind that smashed bones. Some had already signs of beard and I struggled to convince the other teams that they were not in their thirties and grown up, when in fact they were all under sixteen.

"Come on guys, line up all to the baseline," then I went to put an orange cone forty meters away. "Today we do some speed tests, when you hear the whistle, you race up to the cone. Second whistle and run runs up to the end of the field. I don't want to see slackers, indeed, the rule for now on is that we continue until one of you jerk offs vomits its soul." After that it was a lot of whistles and runs.

The boys were working hard, on that front they were admirable.

The first to throw up was Gerardo, a raged little Sicilian with a temper, who played as fly-half. He was also the designated one for the free kicks.

We worked hard on those. We had spent weeks cleaning up his technique. Three steps back, two on the side, no mess. Always the same, always the same length. He had to become an automatism, every kick a goal. It also served as discipline because I threw every game the referee would throw him out of because of his temper.

The one who didn't seem to have any problem was the prop, Giambattista. He had more traction than a Lamborghini tractor and they sure fed him with live cows at home; he was about one hundred and ten kilos of muscle and people would be afraid of him, even in the major league. Perhaps he was the only one that could go all the way to the major league, if it weren't for the fact that he was a deaf-mute. This suited us fine; with that physique he could carry the ball forward and it would take five opposing players to knock him down, but it was not without mix ups. Every now and then he turned to look at me for instructions. I gave him as a *foster child* to Gerardo, who was, as far as I was concerned, the coach on the field. Gerardo kept insulting him all the time, swearing in Sicilian, sure he couldn't be heard a thing, and get away with it, but all in all he was a decent guy.

"Ok guys, now that you are warm let's move the ball around. Come on, everybody in a row, run to the other side of the field and pass the damn ball."

They hated the training. After running they would do push ups, other gruesome exercises, and work on the scrum. We had a nice new shiny machinery for that, an unaware donation from Bishop Filiberto.

After about forty minutes of sweat, it finally came the moment for some action, and at that point they were all ready to beat the crap out of each other. I didn't bother to give them instructions during the game, I was not that sort of control freak trainer. I let them do what they wanted. Twice a week we were training on tactics but then it would be their job to put them into practice during the game. It was a crossroad to the concept of responsibility. I didn't want to be asked what to do at every moment; I gave them the information, the training tactics and during the game it would be up to them. Unless they started to do some shitty play one after another. They knew it and they had become proud of it, if Venanzio says nothing we're doing the right thing, if he starts swearing like a dockland worker on strike, we're in trouble.

It was towards the end of the second half when the incident happened.

The smack could be compared to the one

made by the Titanic clashing against the iceberg, the explosion of the Hindenburg in New Jersey, Wile E. Coyote when he falls into a canyon.

Tommaso, the second prop, and Giambattista collided right on the half field line, a couple of meters away from where I was standing. Is there an expression to describe the noise of crushed collar bones, broken clavicles and ribs that go to hell? A heinous crack followed by a double thud on the ground. Fifteen thousand euro in my pocket from the website. I should have spent them to have some decent grass put on the oratory rugby pitch, which by now was all bare earth. During the winter it became an indescribable quagmire, good for the Navy Seals recruits, but inadequate to play rugby. They formed puddles that looked like lakes. Damn! I had to say goodbye to the money, I made my mind up. If the guys kept playing that well, they would deserve to do it on some decent grass. I just didn't feel right in ripping them off too.

"Giambattista, are you okay?" I asked looking at the young boy from top to bottom. No answer.

He laid down with his face in the dirt and when he turned he looked like a clay statue.

"HOT A WHACK, HATHER ENANZIO", he said without getting up from the ground. OK, at least he spoke, maybe he didn't break his neck, no ambulances nor coroner needed.

"Come on, get up. For today you have done enough, go and get changed." He stared at my lips but I wasn't sure he had understood.

"ENOUGH FOR TODAY" I said chanting the words and hoping he could read my lips, "CHANGING ROOM!" I spat on my hand and tried to remove all that dirt from his mouth and ears. OK, I should have used a sponge, but at that time I was too worried that someone had broken his neck.

"Ouch, I got an electric shock," said Giambattista.

It was supposed to sound like "I hot eletic hockd," but for some reason he pronounced the phrase correctly. Mysteries of rugby accidents. "Locker room!" I repeated and the young boy walked in slow steps into the building.

Tommaso, the other prop, was also shaken but not in bad shape. "You too, go take a shower."

And then I called the others.

"End of fun! The lesson for today is: beat the crap out of your opponent on Sunday because otherwise they'll take you off the field on a stretcher."

It was not a great speech, I knew I could do better, but I was shocked. I didn't follow them in the locker room, I never did. I had several flaws but at least I wasn't a pervert.

CHAPTER 17

"Hello Yaron, Venanzio speaking."

Yaron Rabinovich was a torah scholar and an old acquaintance, since before I became a priest. We met when we were twenty years old and from that point on we became friends. We didn't keep in touch often lately, but a phone call every few months was all we needed to catch up on the latest happenings, from both sides.

It seemed a cliché but Yaron was the king of stinginess, once he dragged me to eat out in a crappy place in a seedy area just because it was cheap. If I remember correctly we were served eels marinated in a sewage and floppy chips. The arsehole praised that as sublime food.

"Ah finally you call back. I'm always the one calling you," said Yaron. It was not true. Those rare times he called me he did it from the office, to save money on his utility bills.

"What can I say, I have a busy life. Look I'm calling because I have in my hand the opportunity of the century: a parishioner left me a whole set of special, high precision pliers and I immediately thought of you. You know, you could use them to pinch pennies, your main line of business."

"But thanks. What about you? Still stealing money on behalf of the paedophile Church?" he replied back.

"Whenever I can, but I have to admit being a lost sheep, still I like the old-fashioned pussy. But enough with the pleasantries, I could use some help. Do you have any friend who knows... never mind, stupid question, obviously you know one; I need to get in touch with an expert in antique books."

"Easy to say. It is like to say an expert of cooking. Chinese, French, Italian, what? What kind of books, what period?" asked Yaron.

"An ancient bible made a thousand years ago. Excellent stuff that I would like to have authenticated, or at least have an estimate on the value."

"Ah, not bad. What have you done, did you remove one of the floorboards in the Bareggio's church and found the Templar treasure?" he asked, but in the meantime, I could hear him fiddling around on the computer.

"Something like that."

"We would ask Benjamin Mantovani-Levi who teaches at the University. He's done some valuable research on ancient bibles, he is an expert and he is reliable," said Yaron.

I wonder what he meant by reliable. It was rumoured that Yaron was part of Mossad. One day, before I became a priest he told me, "Change the computer password, the one you got is too simple." The only password I had was the one on the computer at work, an old desktop which weighed about twenty pounds, but when I told him not to tell bullshit he wrote my password on a piece of paper. That scared me because we never talked about my job. Also, he always remained vague on his line of work. As far as I knew he was working for a large financial company; they sent him to non-performing debtors, on behalf of the Bank and, after working on their accounts he came up with either a plan to save the unfortunate company, or tearing it down and then sell the pieces to the highest bidder to repay the debts. Which often belonged to the bank he was working for. Or at least, that was what I had understood. He told me once he went into one of the largest dairy companies in Italy and had silenced the CEO, forcing him to follow his plan for restructuring the company as any other person would talk about the weather or their favourite football team. But I could not take away from my nostrils that smell of

Mossad. He gave me the address, which I wrote on the back of an envelope.

Benjamin met me at his private office, in a 19th century building, *via della Commenda*. No plaque on the door to indicate the study nor a caretaker in sight, so I went up the stairs. Bloody Yaron, he could have at least told me at which floor he was, and instead had to watch every single name on the doors. I found him on the second floor and I rang a very quiet bell. A good start.

Benjamin opened the door; a man in his fifties with thick glasses and a combover of hair that would have made Donald Trump envious. His however were grey peppered and seemed a little greasy.

"I was expecting you, Father Venanzio, please, come in."

I had suspected that the study was a private apartment and that in fact the good Benjamin used a room for office matters, but I was wrong. The interior looked like an old library made of dark wood and smelled of ancient paper. It reminded me of a notary's office where I had been once. I was still a student at university and one of the girls in the group I attended had invited me "to study" in her aunt's office that afternoon. Paola, if I remember correctly the name, the year before she had got engaged to an idiot redhead, for reasons that were unknown to me yet. The invitation came all of a sudden, one day we found ourselves alone in the library and I had willingly accepted her invite. After all that brunette had the most beautiful arse in the university; many would have deemed too big, but that was a typical mistake of youth. They all compared the girls with models I had in mind, such as Schiffer and Herzigová while I moved on, I was fascinated, bewildered by that piece of equipment. I did nothing else but stare at that Shakira arse all the time, the kind that will hypnotise you and you cannot take your eyes off. The hips don't lie. But when you're young you also create silly barriers, such as not flirting with the friend's girlfriend. Luckily she had thought otherwise.

I followed Benjamin to his desk, then I opened my old leather bag and took out the Bible. I had it wrapped in a cloth as you do with stolen goods. Benjamin wore a pair of white gloves, removed the cloth and began to study the book. One page at a time.

"Fine specimen that you have here," he said.

I tarried from commenting, I wanted to ask how much is it worth? But in certain things, patience was key.

"Ah, here it is," he mumbled, he spoke to himself and when he was satisfied, he closed the heavy book. "Here is a copy of the Bible made by the Parisian School of Johannes Grusch, probably made around 1250 with an approximate value of two hundred thousand euro," said Benjamin. I was starting to salivate. "That is, if it wasn't a fake. And this one is."

"What do mean a fake? Take a better look."

"I looked at it. It's almost impossible to spot, but I've evaluated an equal one twenty years ago. There was little doubt then and there are none today. Someone has spent years to create these copies; it is a very small market but also very lucrative."

Poof! My dream had vanished in a flash. I turned the Bible into my direction, I opened. It was a masterpiece.

"Do not let yourself be fooled, it smells like a book that has been in a church for nearly a millennium, but I assure you that this is not the case. And that patina of grease is not due to thousands of hands that browsed it. It was made by a professional who knew what he was doing; using chestnut oil to recreate that patina is an art in itself. If I hadn't had previous experience, when we even did chemical analysis of colours, it would have fooled me. Specifically, you see this blue? Simply this substance did not exist in 1200. Wait..."

He left the room and returned with a wooden box. He pulled from a drawer a page, nearly equal to those that I had under my eyes. "This was done by the school of Grusch and it is an original. I put one on the side of the other side and to my untrained eye they seemed identical.

"They look absolutely the same to me."

"And they are. The senses do tell a story, the smell of an old book, the wear, maybe obtained with incandescent lamps, the colours slightly faded, the worn parchment, but trust me, it's all a trick to make you believe a story that is untrue. In front of a book made with such great skill you want to believe it's original."

And he had me fooled, I walked right into that and I thought I had found a treasure. "What happened to the other Bible, that false one, I mean?"

"That one I got it. The customer has spent a hefty sum to be sure to buy an original, and the seller did not know what to do with a fake. When the seller realised he had a fake he wanted to destroy it. "

"Why didn't he do that?"

"Dear Father Venanzio, it might be a fake, but it remains a work of art nonetheless."

Now taken from despondency, I asked "could you take a look at these other books?" I took from the bag the two remaining books I had borrowed from the Baldacci.

"Hmm, what do we have here?" said Benjamin watching the two tomes "A *Decades Historiae Romanae di Tito Livio*, a first-rate incunabulum of late fifteenth century tabula and a *Galliae tabula Geographica* from the sixteen century. Let me see... Ah, yes. These are original. A great find, my dear Venanzio. Do you have anything else?"

"How much are they worth?"

"The first ten thousand euro and I would say this," he said, pointing to the *Galliae*, "probably could be sold for twenty thousand euro, maybe a little more."

I took the partial listing that Peter had prepared. "These are some other books belonging to a private library."

Benjamin read the titles fast and authors. "If you want to bring them here, I have contacts among private collectors who might be interested, obviously I would like to have a commission, but we could be talking about a lot of money."

Of course. Yay!

CHAPTER 18

I was on par; at least I wasn't missing out big time. An App in development, a website that was raising money, selling Peter as a sex slave to the highest bidder, and a number of books in the library of the Baldacci lady that were originals. The areas of focus were the Bible, which had proved to be a hoax, the Rugby team that needed improvement and another couple of things.

I called the Bishop.

"Good morning your Holiness."

"Venanzio, his Excellency is just fine. Did you saw the news today? Two other priests arrested; this story is getting out from our hands. And we moved those priests away a couple of times already."

So he knew, the bastard. I was not surprised; if one of those had come to confess to me, relying on silence, the Bishop should have been in the know.

"But why did you call me?" he continued.

"You know, it's about that ancient Bible, I could bring it to you in a couple of days, the only problem is the price because the owner has set themselves on the amount of two hundred thousand euro and she doesn't want to change her mind. I tried to persuade her to make a donation, we would have dedicated an entire area in the Church to her family, or renamed the rugby field in the name of her husband, but nothing."

"About that, let's meet next week. I came to know that we've got a copy in the Vatican archives and I've asked them to send it to me. Of course, there will also be an expert to evaluate its authenticity. In these things you can never be too careful."

Shit! No, fuck, fuck, fuck! I had hoped that the old fart would fall in love with that bloody bible at first sight and fork out the money without blinking. Hofstadter was right with his law: it always takes more than you expect, even taking into account Hofstadter's law. A marvel of recursion.

"Alright next week then," I said. I had nothing else to add, but I was more determined than ever to rip him off. What I would do, I wasn't sure yet.

It was at that moment that Simonetta arrived.

"Father Venanzio, I'm pregnant!"

Holy Fuck, who in hell convinced me to pursue a career as a priest? Shit and buggery, when it rained, it poured.

"I BET YOU CAN'T PASS THIS ONE AS VIRGINAL CONCEPTION," said the voice of God. There was a slight hint of humour in his voice.

"That is still to be seen," I said.

"Of course I'm pregnant! My period is late and I even took the test."

"No, no, I was talking to myself."

"HA! PURE DELUSIONS OF GRANDEUR. YOU ARE TALKING TO GOD, NOT TO YOURSELF."

God, you just sit silently all day, there are millions of faithful waiting for your fucking word. Don't you have anything else to do? No chosen people to free today? No creation of new animals? Ribs to be extracted? There is a butcher around the corner making a discount, ten ribs eight euro.

I continued, "but are you sure?"

"Of course I'm sure. I'm late and I even peed on the thingy. Look: the plus sign is evident. Pos-i-tive."

I thought it over for a moment and indeed I hadn't used any protection, it was against the dictates of the Church and then with the condom I could not feel anything.

"See, you just said the right word, *late*. Do

you know how many times these false alarms happen?"

Saints Ogino and Knaus, please save me.

"TRY TO ASK HER YOU IF YOU'RE THE FATHER," suggested the voice of God.

There was already one priest in the hospital, beaten to pulp, I didn't want to be the second one.

"Simonetta, honestly. What future could I give to that creature? I'm a priest, and if people get to know I won't even be that anymore. You'd end up with a guy without a job as the father of the creature, a homeless man forced to live under bridges because I wouldn't even have money to buy diapers."

"Ah, you're pulling out? Bastard! What am I supposed to do?"

"Maybe find a good father to this creature who, let us not forget, is a gift from God. There's nobody that could be a good candidate? I don't know, a colleague, a friend. It could be a seven-month baby born, it happens, it would not be something unheard before."

"Asshole!"

"Think About It, Simonetta. I know that right now you're upset ..."

"AND PREGNANT! AND PISSED OFF. DO

YOU KNOW HOW MANY HORMONES ARE UNLEASHING WITHIN THE POOR THING NOW?"

"... upset, I was saying, and that perhaps the desire for revenge might make its way into your heart now. But what would it change? What future would there be for us?"

"Asshole!"

"SHE IS NOT COMPLETELY WRONG."

"Think about it, find a good guy, someone who can be a good family man."

Simonetta was furious and perhaps was going to kill me in that moment, but then she began to cry. I tried to comfort her but she wouldn't hear any of it. With good reason. If I was in her shoes, I would have picked up a baseball bat; not mine, which by now was sailing briskly down the Ticino river.

God, save me from this story and I swear to shag only those who are married. If they get pregnant, the father is easily found.

"I HAVE TO THINK IT OVER."

Right, think about it, from the top of your glory.

Nothing. From Simonetta came just insults in response to my attempts to persuade her, but maybe I had managed to convince her. I whispered reasonable words, it was hard not to listen to the voice of reason. Let her find an idiot. She was very pretty, it wouldn't take much to fool someone.

Finally she left, thankfully without breaking anything. I did not have time to breathe a sigh of relief when the telephone rang. It was Peter.

"Venanzio, you have to come here by the Baldacci's. I mean, NOW!"

"What happened, did they find out who you are?"

"Venanzio, make it quick, I can't talk on the phone. Hurry up!"

And then he hung up.

Jesus Christ, as if I wasn't in deep shit already.

CHAPTER 19

Somewhere between the Church and the Baldacci's house I thought about the most likely reason to cause such havoc. First and foremost that Fiammetta, for some reason, went to find the Baldacci and had discovered "the negro".

"Chief Oguntoye, what are you doing here?"

"But no, this is the distinguished Oxford professor Dr. Oguntoye," would answer the Baldacci lady.

"When he was shagging me, last week, he was dressed as an African chieftain ..."

"And now he is evaluating all those ancient books in my husband's library..."

A call to Commissioner Toscani would follow; an armoured cab ride to the Opera prison for me and Peter. Then the extradition for my partner in crime. I didn't intend to lose my arse virginity in jail. At the first sign of flashing lights, I would have driven straight onto the motorway, destination Switzerland. I would find a place as a priest of a small mountain village in the Canton of Ticino. It wouldn't be too bad.

Or maybe the Baldacci, or worse, Filippa

went for a ride on my fake website and had seen chieftain Oguntoye on display, and his jewels. No, that couldn't happen, I didn't upload the photos I had shown to Fiammetta.

Maybe they had gone to Milan and had seen him selling fake handbags. If Peter hadn't opened his mouth, that could be sorted out. They are blacks, Mrs Baldacci, they all look alike, like the Chinese. I could get away with the two old ladies, but not with Filippa, she wasn't completely dumb.

"DO NOT ASK FOR HELP, I WASH MY HANDS."

"Try to tell your son that sentence and then see what happens."

"IT IS PRECISELY THE POINT."

"The point of what? I'm here as a defender of the faith, I'm not here trying to comb dolls or spot cleaning jaguars. Ah, no, I understand the approach, let us arm ourselves and *you* go, the *hidden God* of Father Giussani and other fundamentalists. If all goes well, you take the credit, if things go pear shape you're the hidden God. Nice job and risk-free you have."

I parked in front of the Baldacci's house and I knocked on the door.

"What's happening," I asked Peter, who had come to open it.

"Watch for yourself."

I walked down the hall till the main room and, there they were the Pina, the Gina and Filippa. The last one also standing.

"Father Venanzio! It's a miracle," said Mrs Pina, "look, she can stand on her feet."

I looked at Peter who in turn showed me an idiotic face.

"Filippa, what's going on?"

"I can't explain it. For several days I felt a tingling in my legs and today, by chance, I tried to move them. And they would answer, right Peter? They moved, Father Venanzio." The woman was absolutely surprised, of that there was no doubt. I say, from a wheelchair to standing like that. I would have had a heart attack if it happened to me.

"What the fuck did you do?" I asked Peter in a whisper, "Did you show her the black magic wand you have between your legs? Did you do a spell Harry Potter's style? *Erection patronum*? *Engorgio drillbittus*? *Bayonet eiaculatio*?"

"Venanzio, don't be an asshole, it isn't the time," whispered back Peter.

"Do you believe in miracles?"

"And we gave clear miracles to Jesus, the son of Mary, and strengthened him with the Holy Spirit," cited Peter by memory.

"As long as it is not, *'I fashion for you out of clay the likeness of a bird, and I breathe into it and it is a bird'* A cock, in your case. I read recently of this new treatment: two pills before and after meals of Dickulin B12 and…"

"Shut the fuck up for once; Filippa is a decent girl! " he said testily.

"Or maybe it was the Penetril." And then turning to the crowd, "Filippa, you never had signs before of a possible healing?"

"Absolutely not! I have the x-ray in my room, the doctors were adamant, I wouldn't walk again."

"It's a miracle," said Gina.

"It's a miracle," said Pina.

"We must call the Bishop," said Gina.

Like hell! The Bishop would have met the two old ladies, he would have convinced them right and then to give up the fake Bible for free and end of the story. Probably along with many other books in the library. When he wanted, the shark, he knew what to do. And then he would blow the whistle on Peter in a flash: he could pass for an expert in front of the Baldacci, but the Bishop was an authority on ancient books.

And then the newspapers. They would come immediately, ready to take pictures, to investigate. A picture of Peter in the paper, given that he had been present at the event would be a ruin. Fiammetta would recognize him, there would be an investigation, they would discovered that he was an illegal immigrant. At a minimum deportation. And then it would be my turn: I was the one who made the introduction. Facing the Commissioner Toscani was something I would have rather avoided.

Filippa returned with a folder full of health records, which she put on the table. We passed each other x-rays as if we were in *Doctor House'* hospital, *come on guys differential diagnosis, and no, it's not Lupus*. We understood some of what we were reading, maybe we could have done a bit of speculation, but that wasn't the case.

"We need to be cautious with these things," I said. I had to shut down the enthusiasm straight away. "You know, Mrs. Pina, how many healings were not recognized by the Church as miracles? We must investigate, these things take years. You have to employ scholars that cost a lot of money."

"It's a miracle," said Gina.

"It's a miracle," said Pina.

"I want to go for an ice cream," said Filippa, "I want to walk, to feel alive again. Peter, would you mind accompanying me? I'm still a little shaky on my legs."

"Of course, gladly," said back my buddy grabbing her by her arm. The two ladies didn't bat an eyelid to the fact that "the negro" had, as a matter of fact, bagged a first date with Filippa.

Fuck, fuck, fuck! I handed over twenty euro to Peter without being seen. It wasn't good to go to an ice cream parlour and have no means to pay. Especially when you were supposed to come from Oxford.

"We shall call the newspapers," said Gina.

"Ladies, ladies. Let's sit down and pray before making hasty decisions." Bloody Peter, he left me alone to deal with the two women. It would take time to convince the two beguines.

CHAPTER 20

I had to pull Peter out from that situation. I needed more time to lead my schemes to a conclusion.

The cataloguing work was finished, perhaps we lacked some books, but it wouldn't make much difference. Peter and Filippa returned soon after, with two giant ice cream cones, they looked like Peynet lovers. What a shame.

"Peter, I need the list of the books *ipso facto*, immediately. With this mess we have no time to lose."

"Venanzio, aren't you freaking out a bit too much? With what just happened ..."

"Peter, don't be a dick and trust me. When did I ever get you into trouble?"

"Come to think of it, there was that time when ...

"OK, I got it, I got it! Look, we need to move those books before this thing of the miracle attracts too much attention."

We went to the library and turned on the computer then moved the file to my phone.

Thankfully the good Benjamin had been busy. A few minutes later I got a call saying that there were already some forty buyers ready to pay money. We had found a treasure in that library. Yaron himself was interested and had helped to spread the word.

"Father Venanzio," said Benjamin, "the market is in turmoil. They call me every hour to know when they can see the books. These collectors are like that: they wait for years, patient, that one of these books might surface and then go wild as sharks when they smell blood. We cannot wait any longer, when can we start selling? By the way, I sent back the list with an estimated price for each book; of course you have to consider my commission." Of course.

I thought for a moment. "Ok, keep them warm. I have a matter to deal with but I'll call you soon, hopefully with good news."

"AND THEN YOU SAY THAT MIRACLES DON'T HAPPEN," said the voice of God.

"This is not the time now. I'll talk to you later," I muttered.

"Mrs Baldacci," I said coming back in the living room, "we have good news."

All the faces turned in my direction.

"We have found buyers for your husband's library, but we can't waste time. This Saturday we should do an auction, here at home. There will be a lot of people but I'm sure we can sell most of the books."

"But how do we do it? There has just been a miracle in this house..." said Gina.

"A house that you will lose if we don't move quickly. These buyers will not wait for a long time, you know how collectors are. They keep collecting. If they don't spend money here, they're going to buy somewhere else. There is no time to lose."

"We trust you," said Mrs Gina. Good woman.

I walked away a few paces and I called Benjamin. "We are on track for this Saturday. Invite them all, I'll send you a text message with the address. Ah, we only accept cashier's cheques or cash. No regular cheques, bills of exchange, promises of bank transfers." I thought about Peter and then I added, "you show the money, you get to see the camel."

"All right. See, cashier's cheques today must have a nominee. Rules introduced by article 2 of Decree-Law 13 August 2011 # 138, in amending article 49 of legislative decree 21 November 2007 # 231."

"What do you mean they should have a nominee? What the hell are you, Wikipedia, that you cite me decrees?" In fact, though I hadn't seen a cashier's cheques in centuries.

Maybe he was right.

Peter was watching me with an evil eye. Fuck, fuck, fuck. "Ok, cheques made payable to Giuseppina Baldacci."

Bloody blimey, a disproportionate amount of euro that went to hell. I still had the fake Bible though and maybe I could make off with a briefcase full of cash.

I hung up the phone and went back to the living room.

"Mrs. Pina, we are on track for Saturday."

"But Father Venanzio, and the miracle?"

"Mrs. Pina, please stop bothering me with this story about the miracle. That must be verified. Here," I said transferring the file on that Benjamin had sent me on the computer, "this is an estimate of the books you have in the library."

Mrs Pina put on her glasses and began to read. Nearby, Gina had done the same and standing from behind, Filippa.

"Three hundred thousand euro? It's another miracle," said Pina.

"It's another miracle," said Gina.

It was Commissioner Toscani's fault I got rid of my baseball bat. How could I remove from their heads that story about the miracle? Peter looked at me and smiled.

"Look, I know you're excited at the moment, but this story should be analysed with a clear head. If you start to talk left, right and centre about a *possible* miracle, you would find journalists outside the door. The gentlemen interested in buying your books are wealthy people, but also individuals who care about their privacy."

I could feel the wheels turning in their heads.

"If they see reporters, they get scared," said Gina.

"And if they get scared they don't buy," said Pina.

"Right," I said just to put the icing on the cake. "They don't want to show the world how they spend their money. I say, tens of thousands of euro for a book? How many charities could be helped with that kind of money? It would harm their image and they would prefer to avoid being seen."

"We must pass the miracle under silence," said Pina.

Brave women. When challenged, they understood things. I just had to present the facts under the right light.

"So, how about this: the miracle does not happen until after the auction. Indeed, perhaps it is better to push through another week. The auction is Saturday, so you would find yourself with a lot of cash in the house and no chance to deposit the money in the bank. With all the criminals that are out there, you have to pass this story under wraps."

"You are right, Father Venanzio."

"We could have the auction in the garden. Bernacca said that the weekend will be sunny."

Edmondo Bernacca, an Air Force General and meteorologist, had been dead for at least twenty years. He hosted the weather forecast on television in the sixties and then he retired. But for Mrs Pina anyone who read the weather forecast on television, even nowadays, was a *Bernacca*.

"Perfect. Peter, if you want to help the ladies with the logistics, I have errands to run. See you tonight."

"Certainly Venanzio, leave it to me."

When I was by the door, I said to Peter "you know what's going on, right, if this story about the miracle gets out?"

'"Of course."

"Put a lid on the whole affair, be the voice of reason for these two poor women. Otherwise, next week you have to really go for the lion hunt."

"There is no need to remind me. See you tonight."

I climbed in the car but I did not turn on the engine immediately. Jesus Christ, maybe we had avoided troubles, but who knew what might have happened from there to Saturday.

CHAPTER 21

I had a copy of the *Corriere della Sera* open on my desk. On the front page, a photo of Commissioner Toscani and the series of arrests that he had made that week. The article told of the progress so far: after the arrests in Bareggio and Father Zambrini comatose, the Commissioner had been busy. Four other priests were jailed and another dozen had received warrant notices. The Commissioner wasn't keen to disclose his late findings, the investigation was still in progress in what was called *Operation Clean Confessional* but he let it be understood that he was adopting a zero-tolerance policy. The computer division of the police were tracking down evidence on the internet, the first witnesses were coming forward. They still didn't know who sent Zambrini to the hospital but the commissioner suspected one of the other priests in that circle to silence him, without doubt.

"Good morning, Benjamin, Venanzio speaking."

"Hello Venanzio, is everything in order?" he asked on the other end of the phone.

"Yes of course. Saturday will be a great day.

I'm calling to ask you a favour. That Grusch Bible you showed me, could you lend it to me for a few days?"

Silence.

"Yes, no problem, but I told you it was another fake. What are you thinking?"

How could I explain? I couldn't say for sure what I had in mind either.

"I'm getting interested. I simply want to see them both next to each other to better understand who could do such a thing. A mere curiosity. I swear I won't damage your copy."

"Of course, take it for as long as you like. If it was any other book I would have refused of course, you know, they are delicate."

"Don't worry. See you in the afternoon."

"See you later."

Half of the plan I had in mind was in the making. Now came the tricky part. I searched for a number on my address book.

I dialled the number from the landline in my office. "Sister Germana, hello, I'm Father Venanzio."

"Ah, Venanzio, how are you? The Bishop is out of the office today."

"What a shame, there was something important I wanted to discuss. But how are you Germana, I heard that you came back to the Bishop's office recently, how many years have passed, two, three?"

"Two long years. I was in the Convent of the merciful Sisters of the holy and televised heart of Jesus and the saints Seat-eth and Boot-eth."

That was the equivalent of Wandsworth for a nun, or Riccione for us priests. From what I saw, differently from our Bishop, Toscani much preferred to send priests to the Opera prison. Who knows what nasty thing she had done to deserve two entire years in that place.

"I had a dear sister that has been there. A slight detour from the path of our Lord, you know? She served with Father Gerard, of the order of the Pilgrims of the Bloody Kneecap, those who walk the path to Compostela on their knees. Along the way, they caught them behind a bush; Father Gerard had decided not to limit itself to the anointing of the knees. The poor sister got caught too, on her knees blowing in Father Gerard's member as if it was a flute. Someone likened the scene to a Eurovision song contest singer who held the microphone a little too close to her mouth ..."

"God have mercy on them," she said, annoyed. No, that was not working. Maybe I was looking at it from the wrong angle. I continued.

"And obviously the case of Sister Ivanka, Repentant of the convent of the Ursulines of the Stolid Denied Member of the Pisan Redentore order. Oddly, that order runs a girl's boarding school in Switzerland. Who knows why. But let's not digress, Sister Ivanka used the old methods, lashes on the poor students' bum."

"Oh my God, what happened?"

This time I had hit the jackpot.

"Sister Ivanka firmly believes that a young mind should be shaped, with the rod if necessary."

"Don't tell me."

"I tell you, I tell you. That College was not a simple place, dear Germana. All daughters of wealthy entrepreneurs, spoiled brat girls since their childhood, used to live in luxury. Arrogant girls and full of pride."

"Hardly the rich shall enter the Kingdom of heaven" Sister Germana quoted.

"That's right. And what better way to bring those little pests on the straight and narrow? Don't get me wrong, Sister Ivanka is very patient, but sometimes the little rebels went over the thin line that exists between being teenagers and end up on the wrong path. In those cases, Sister Ivanka invited, no, better, ordered one of the young pests to follow her in her studio. In this politically correct world, we don't accept corporal punishment any more, but certain methods are still the most effective."

You couldn't hear a pin drop on the other end of the phone. You wouldn't hear it anyway over the phone, but in fact, Sister Germana was in religious silence. Finally, she added, with a feeble voice, "and then what happened."

"There was this Lucrezia, the name in itself will make you understand that she was a lost soul. Sister Ivanka ordered her to get on all fours, she lowered her panties and with a ruler she struck her repeatedly on her butt. You know, those youngsters have firm flesh, and the rebel gave no sign of repentance. I've always said that Sister Ivanka is too good, but finally she realized her mistake and used a whip. Only with pain we can effectively purge our sins. The young sinner screamed but sometimes you are never sure of their true repentance, they might fake, for which Sister Ivanka decided to do an experiment."

"An experiment?"

"Of course. As you know, we must flee from pleasure and seek redemption, and that is precisely what Sister Ivanka did. Certainly, it was an unorthodox method, but that has its own reasoning."

On the other end of the phone you could hear a slight noise and squeaks. I imagined Sister Germana, legs propped on the desk, intent to dig deep between the skirts. It would be a pretty sight, the nun was in her 30s, pretty and used a tight cloth, every time I went to visit the Bishop, I watched all those curves and dreamed.

"I don't understand, Father Venanzio."

"Oh, it's all very simple. Sister Ivanka sat on a couch in her study and asked the girl to lay on the nun's legs. The same position you might want to use to spank a naughty child, and believe me, that girl was naughty. To waive at pleasure, first you must know it, therefore our sister took care of stroking the young girl between her legs. A horrible job but one that needed to be done. Can you imagine, Sister Germana, having a firm and pale bum just in front of you, having to reluctantly caress it, explore those still unripe cavities with your fingers? It is a daunting task, because you would not caress her like you would with a pet. No, you will have to start stroking those pale legs and then move up slowly, until you reach the pubic hair. Gentle strokes that then become firmer and firmer.

"I imagine, I imagine."

"Sister Ivanka is very passionate about her duties, a wholehearted soldier of God. On those occasions she stroked the private parts of that arrogant girl and nothing could stop her. She moistened her fingers in order to make them slide better on the young girl's clitoris, she would penetrate her gently but firmly in all her orifices, because to waive the pleasures of the flesh, you have to know it first. When that young, Lucrezia, cried out her orgasm, only then sister Ivanka lowered the whip, not a moment before. There is an art in corporal punishment, don't wait too long after you have received pleasure. Orgasm, followed by a strike. You know, Sister Germana, you don't need to use a riding crop, a nice little rap on the buttocks, bare handed, is enough. Sister Ivanka always said it was better to alternate the two tactics: the wider whack delivered with the bare hand and the narrow, more intense one of the whip. Whack! Those naughty arses would learn how to stay hidden from sight. And then she would start again: a new pleasure would follow another punishment. Orgasm, whipping."

"As with Pavlov's geese," said my interlocutor.

"Dogs."

"What did you say?"

"Pavlov was the one training dogs. The geese are those of the Capitol Hills in Rome, but don't make me lose my train of thoughts, Sister Germana. As I said, this Lucrezia was a rogue one. She was just eighteen years old but she had already discovered the pleasures of the flesh: sister Ivanka realised that during one of her explorations that the young girl was no longer a virgin. This gave her reason to change approach, by no longer using her fingers only but with vibrators that she had confiscated during her long career. Do you know how to use a vibrator, Sister Germana?"

"I don't know certain things, "said Sister Germana between groans and sighs. I went deep into the technicalities of such objects. The clitoral stimulator, the various shapes and sizes, vibration, rotation, gyroscopes and so on and so forth.

It was during the description of squeezed nipples, students made to walk on all fours and other tortures that Sister Germana groaned.

"The poor thing was then redeemed?" she

asked finally, still panting.

"The Lucrezia girl? Of course. She is now a faithful soul; unfortunately someone ratted on her and sister Ivanka was, shall we say, unfairly punished. I'm still in touch with her, and if you want, I could arrange a meeting. Like I said, atone for their sins through the physical pain purifies the soul. Maybe if you come here in Bareggio in the near future, I could give you confession and Sister Ivanka might deliver the penance."

"I think we can do that."

"Next weekend?"

"Of course; it will be, shall we say... interesting."

"See, Sister Germana, you will feel as if your soul had been cleansed, trust me. By the way, I'd have to see the Bishop on Tuesday. I know that he requested an expert in old Bibles directly from the Vatican."

"Ah sure, Father Gregacci. He will arrive in Milan on Monday night, I took care of booking his hotel."

"And where did you book?"

"The hotel Bulgari, why?"

"Ah, an excellent treatment, I see you've made the right choice. Simple curiosity."

"See you next weekend, for that confession?"

asked Sister Germana, anxiously.

"Of course, you are welcome. Come in the morning so you will have time to get to know Sister Ivanka."

Where the hell did I put my vitamins? Well, that was a good start to the morning. *Perpetua, prepare a massive eggnog.*

CHAPTER 22

The Baldacci sisters had been busy. At the entrance there were drinks, pretzels, homemade cakes, and the same could be said of the garden. It seemed like I entered the summer home of Sotheby's. I had obviously given my contribution by bringing several chairs from the parish, a microphone and a speaker. Peter would handle the auction and Filippa would have been his assistant, showing the books when called.

Obviously, the guests could see the books they were interested in upfront in the library, under careful supervision of Mrs Gina and Pina.

Luxury cars were parked all the way on the main road and for the taxi drivers it was an early Christmas. Anyone who had passed nearby might have thought of a wedding in style.

I was gobbling apple pie and orange soda. I could have drank a Corona instead but it appeared that Mrs Baldacci did not appreciate the Mexican nectar, despite my hints on the matter. Maybe they were sympathisers of Trump.

Peter wore a pinstripe suit, white shirt and pink tie. I didn't remember at that time which dead man that suit belonged to, but Peter looked amazing in it.

We had arranged everything perfectly. We didn't put the most expensive books at the beginning, that would have been a strategic error that could leave us with a lot of unsold items. Better alternating, some recent first editions, then an important work, then other cheaper books and then another important book.

We had to rip them off big time.

"Good morning and welcome," announced Peter. "You can find the catalogue (an Excel handout) on that table, the auction will begin in 15 minutes."

Well done Peter, he was managing the lot professionally. Every now and then he looked in the direction of Filippa, who in turn threw glances of encouragement. My personal slave who played the Peynet lover. There was no religion anymore.

I didn't have much else to do and that Saturday I was expecting Sister Germana and Sister Ivanka.

Actually, Ivanka was not a nun, but a Russian shameless whore that I had met some time ago. She made me earn brownie points with the commissioner Toscani by providing conclusive evidence regarding a gang who was trafficking in women from the Eastern Europe. Ivanka now didn't work on the side of the street anymore, she had said no to those dastardly performances for a few euro and a quickie consumed in a car. Now she was a high-class hooker in the Centre of Milan and she almost had more money than Zuckemberg. She had become a pussy oligarch but, as rarely happens, she had never forgotten her real friends.

For the occasion I hadn't even had to ransack the sacristy, Ivanka came equipped with all the necessary. I asked her to give up the latex nun dress, which would have aroused suspicions, and so she came wearing a Daughters of Charity of Saint Vincent de Paul nun dress, including the huge cornette. Christ, that headwear resembled a giant origami. It was no longer used, not in the past half of a century, but it would still be in line with the character of Sister Ivanka, respectful of traditions.

In the big bag she carried with her, there were several instruments of torture, including riding crops, a carpet beater made of vimini, cats with an unspecified number of tails, nipple tweezers, masks, arse-beads (which for sure had a lot more technical, high-toned name), anal plug, vibrators in all shapes, sizes and characteristics.

"Jesus Christ, Ivanka, we have one afternoon, it's not that we have to do a remake of the *Shades*. We are in a sacristy, not in Guantanamo."

Ivanka was relaxed on the armchair of my studio and she was smoking a cigarette. Now, if you've never seen a Russian chick dressed as a nun while she smokes, you haven't lived. She was giving me a boner already. "You said that she is a real nun, Da?"

"Da, Da. So slow it down, don't push too hard."

"I am a professional, what do you think? I know what needs to be done."

Thank goodness, because at that point I wasn't sure, on certain things you could never know. It was my fault, I sometimes had ideas that seemed brilliant on paper, but they could turn into disasters in a moment. What if Sister Germana backed out? Maybe she liked to get excited over the phone but when facing the harsh reality she could run like hell. Better not to think about it, I told myself, and I opened a bottle of Corona.

And then there was the choice of venue. It would have turned me on doing it on the altar, imagining the faithful in religious silence, but maybe Sister Germana had some objections. No, my office was the best choice.

I heard a knock at the door.

"May I?" said Sister Germana sticking her head from behind the door.

"Of course, come in. This is Sister Ivanka," I said pointing to my foreign guest. Ivanka blew out the cigarette smoke and, she stood up from the armchair very slowly to shake hands with Sister Germana. "Nice to meet you."

Sister Germana looked at me shocked. Ivanka was a leggy Valkyrie six feet high, to which it was necessary to add five inches due to the stilettos she was wearing. Not to consider the cornette she had on her head. She was hot but if someone had tried to imagine the Angel of Death, he would have surely thought about Ivanka in that outfit, *Seal with a righteous kiss a dateless bargain to engrossing death!* said the Bard. Or maybe it was *Shakespeare in love*, the movie.

I had to take matters into my own hands before Sister Germana ran off like hell or, at the very least, was taken by doubts.

"Where had I put my vestments? Ah, here they are. So, let's proceed as follow: now you and I go in the confessional. I will listen very carefully to your sins. Then we will return here in my office for the penance."

"How will Sister Ivanka know which penance ..."

"I will assist her. I'll be the judge of your repentance and I will inform Sister Ivanka when will suffice. Obviously, you, Sister Germana, you might say when you feel truly repented. Sister Ivanka, what do you think?"

"That sin should be purged, that the flesh is weak and I will be the judge of the true repentance of sister Germana." No room for discussion, considering her tone of voice.

Jesus Christ! But I was in the hand of a professional, I just hoped for the best.

"Come on, Sister Germana, please follow me."

The woman looked around, like a caged animal that seeks a way out but then she followed obediently. The confession was relatively short, covering the reasons for her confinement at Wandsworth, pardon to the convent, plus some other mischiefs done in the meanwhile. Nothing that I could repeat due to the sacred seal of the confessional, I am a servant of God after all, but not anything that I hadn't done before myself. Me and the sacrificial lamb set off towards my office.

"All done," I announced to Ivanka. The Valkyrie stood up, turned around Germana as a shark that is considering the next prey and then suddenly ordered, "KNEEL!"

In the meanwhile, I was sitting comfortably on a leather chair. For a while I would have enjoyed the show, the problem would come later. How to introduce my blessed rod into Sister Germana and pass it as expiation of sins? I trusted in Ivanka.

Sister Germana got down on her knees; obey in order to fight the evil one, because with poverty and chastity we wouldn't have gone very far, that afternoon.

Ivanka was not satisfied, so she took Germana by the shoulders and pushed her on all fours. Now, that was a most congenial pose, with her butt facing in my direction. Ivanka made another circle around the victim, you could hear the noise of heels on the wooden floor, some slight creaking but nothing more. Then Ivanka went to her bag, weighing the various instruments of torture. She chose a horse whip, semi-rigid, which she secured to the wrist using strings; with that she lifted

Sister Germana's wide skirts. She was wearing stockings and you could see the lace panties, the buttocks exposed. Ah, interesting. No hint during confession about the sin of vanity. Ivanka gave me a look, she too had noticed the clothing. We should have taken that into account during the punishments. Just to nit-pick, the only downside were Germana's shoes, an abomination, but at least she had shaved her legs, which were smooth and soft to the touch of the whip. I found the cure to impotence; I could bankrupt Pfizer and their Viagra: an Ivanka and a Germana around would make a dead man stiff. My penis throbbed.

WHACK!

Ivanka had lowered the whip on one of Sister Germana's buttocks, who felt the hit. Holy Fuck, Ivanka, take it easy, I thought, don't ruin her.

"Are you repented?"

"Yes, Sister Ivanka."

"LIAR! Repentance doesn't happen so fast. Those are the words of the devil!" She knelt behind Germana and she ran a hand between her thighs. "I know you like this. I know you will not renounce the pleasure of the flesh that easily."

Then she caressed her butt, slipping her hand under her panties.

"Lust is the worst of sins, the most difficult to eradicate." With a sharp tug she lowered her underpants, exposing the woman's sex. "This is the core of sin," Ivanka said swirling a finger on the nun's sex. "There's an easy way to figure out your true repentance." So saying, Ivanka unbuttoned the nun's dress, then she stroked her chest. "Your nipples are hardening, sinner!" and THWACK! Another slap on the butt.

"To give up completely your sins, first you have to understand them," said Ivanka. While Germana was still on all fours, Ivanka had removed the nun's bra, which now lay on the ground near Germana's hands. She pinched a nipple, holding it between the forefinger and the thumb, while the other hand was busy stroking Germana's sex.

Jesus Christ, I wanted to take off my pants and jump onto one of the two, I didn't care which one.

"See, you're getting wet. I knew you weren't truly repented." Ivanka continued to manipulate her until Sister Germana groaned. Fortunately, she had a silent orgasm, I imagined having to explain the cries and moaning as the result of a particularly difficult exorcism.

"Father Venanzio, give me a hand with this sinful woman."

She didn't need to ask twice. Ivanka made Germana lie on her back and then ordered me to hold the nun by the arms. I squatted behind Germana, her face between my legs, and I grabbed her arms. Ivanka was working with her tongue and our poor sister couldn't help but arching her back, pressing her sex against the tough tongue of Ivanka. I saw the nun's breasts move in front of me, I wanted to kiss those tits, grab them, but by this time, I was satisfied to feel my dick rubbing against her face. Ivanka had taken off the cornette and her red hair rested on Germana stomach. I could hear her panting beneath me; praying wouldn't have done any good in trying to stop that Russian tongue licking her. Then Ivanka stood up, wiping the wetness from the mouth with her sleeve and picked up a vibrator. That made Germana moan in a completely different way.

"The devil is inside you; do you renounce the devil? "said Ivanka.

"Ahhh."

"Behold, sinful, enjoy. The soul, if set free is lost in lust, debauchery and depravity!"

Debauchery? Who the hell had prepared the script? Not me.

"Ahhh, I'm coming..."

"Rejoice, because soon you will regret bitterly of your wantonness."

Ivanka grabbed Germana's hips, forcing her to turn around, belly to the ground. Then she picked up the riding whip again and beat her on the buttocks again. I held Germana firmly by the arms, but at every blow the nun bounced, coming into contact with my hard penis. She held my hips, her fingers grasping at my butt while the face thumped rhythmically against my dick. *Come on Ivanka, step aside*, I thought.

After a sequence of slapping on the backside of Sister Germana, Ivanka paused. She got up slowly, heading towards the desk and took a sip of water from a bottle. Better not saying a word, partly also because Sister Germana hadn't moved and still was rubbing her face against my penis. Never complain.

"The flesh is weak" said Ivanka from the top of her six feet. She undid her skirt and dropped it at her feet, revealing two shapely and lightly muscled legs, wrapped in stockings. I admitted it, I had no imagination. The desire to see two women make love, for me to fuck at least one nun was trivial and obvious. I did not care a damn, I could thrive in banality that day.

Ivanka pushed down her panties revealing a red bush on her sex. She sat on my leather chair and, with her legs wide open, openly showing her sex, she said, "Come here, sinner!"

I let her go and Sister Germana approached Ivanka, then she knelt in front of her. Ivanka grabbed her head and pushed her against her sex. Then motioned me to get closer. Certain orders were easy to obey, and I was a good soldier of God. I took off my pants in a hurry. While Sister Germana was licking the Russian's thighs I laid my member against her sex. I slid it inside without resistance; the nun sighed.

I pushed and pushed again, holding her by the wide hips. I could hear her moan, then I heard Ivanka crying her orgasm.

Germana was narrow down there, as I liked it; I felt the walls of her sex rubbing against mine, she was dripping wet. I grabbed her buttocks, pale and firm, and I pushed further against her. I was having sex with a nun; it was not the first and probably would not be the last, but she certainly was the sexiest one. Then I grabbed her breasts from behind and felt her hardened nipples. They quivered at my touch.

Hell, I took off my shirt and I threw myself on top of her. That pushing from behind made her face rubbing against Ivanka's sex once again. Then the Russian stood up from her chair, knelt also and began to kiss her on the mouth. Two nuns, albeit one of them fake, kissing each other gave me new energy. I felt my penis bursting, soon I would have an orgasm. Ivanka took possession of our prey, forcing her to lay on her back. I was faster though and I was over Germana in a flash, a *missionary* style seemed appropriate for the occasion. I saw the disappointment in my partner's face, but tough, first arrived, first served. Ivanka then got down on her knees and bent over the face of sister Germana; she wanted for sure to be licked again. Now I had the nun, the real one, below me, which I was banging out, and faced the white milky arse of Ivanka. Use it or lose it, I thought and when I heard Germana coming for the umpteenth time, I threw myself on the Russian, who I took from behind. Ivanka knew what to do, pushing against my sex but at the same time she didn't forget about Germana. Thankfully, because I at that point didn't know who or where I was anymore. While I was penetrating her, she pushed Germana forward and started fucking her with a purple vibrator;

the handle was in the shape of a crucifix; where the hell had she found such a thing was still to be discovered.

I don't know how long we continued, alternating sex and corporal punishment but at one point I fell exhausted.

Sister Germana laid beside me, panting. I didn't have the energy to do anything else, not that afternoon, but I was hoping that Sister Germana would commit more sins during the following weeks. We put our clothes on in silence, the nun held her gaze to the floor but I could see she was satisfied.

Ivanka was the first to speak, taking away the embarrassment of talking about what just happened. "I'll see you next week. Sin must be fought constantly."

And that was an order neither I nor Sister Germana could disobey.

When they left, I went to the parking lot, where I had left my battered car. My legs were shaking, but I had to check what was happening with the Baldacci.

Dinner time was passed long ago, but that didn't matter and when I got there, I saw that the lights were still on, so I knocked on the door.

"Father Venanzio, come in," said Filippa

coming to open. "We have almost reached two hundred and forty thousand euro, look!"

I was looking. On the table there were cheques, briefcases full of cash, money on the floor. It looked like a bank vault exploded in that very lounge.

Mrs Gina and Pina were excited, the house was saved, they could pay off the debts. After the usual thanks and the unavoidable coffees, they let me go. Peter was already gone.

The problem was, how to make that cash disappear before they took it into the bank? The old ladies were too shaken, they would not have slept that night. I would have to act the following night, the bank would open Monday morning and the two ladies would have hurried to deposit the loot. It wasn't safe to keep all that money in the house.

CHAPTER 23

"So, did you decide on the first name?" I asked the Carusos. Godly people, which didn't lose a mass.

The two looked at each other in the face before speaking. You could see that they had thought it over.

"We would call him Underpontius," said Giuseppe Caruso, full of pride, his wife was holding his hand proudly.

"Underpontius?"

"Yes, like the one mentioned during the Creed: *he suffered Under Pontius Pilate, was crucified, died, and was buried.*"

"It seems to me an excellent choice," I said. "So, we are set for Wednesday, it is eighty euro."

The two paid in cash without blinking an eye, said goodbye and they left.

I went back to look at the contract to fix up the rugby field.

"Father Venanzio!"

Oh boy, George.

"You have forgotten we have a friendly rugby match today, they're waiting for you in the field," said the guy running into my office.

I had other things on my mind. Since Peter had pulled out, refusing to have other meetings with Fiammetta and the other beguines, the level of donations lowered conspicuously. Backing out. A practice which he hadn't imported from his country of origin, he had surely learned it in Italy.

The site still generated some money, but I had also received quotations for redoing the rugby field turf in the meanwhile. The cheapest was five euro and thirty per square meter. Thieves! How did they dare to ask a poor parish like mine to shell out more than twenty thousand euro? I was angry with them and I even called them. I tried to barter and they had responded by talking about soil, peat, sand and slush and mulch, soil depth and mixing chipping of the surface layer previously routed, fertilizing. I had cried it was a theft, threatened to excommunicate them, but nothing. The price did not move.

What I had put aside with the website would be gone, and with it the dream of a motorbike. I definitely could not afford a Harley and with what I had to pay for redoing the field, now I couldn't even afford a used Triumph Bonneville. I put back the Harley brochure in a drawer. Reluctantly. Sighing.

Five thousand and eight hundred euro for a Bonneville with few miles on the clock. Fuck, fuck, fuck!

I had skimmed some money away from the App's final price, but that money was already long gone. I promised myself to use the money I got from the website to redo the rugby field. I wasn't done yet, there were still a couple of projects going on.

I stood up and I followed George.

The opponents was the Inveruno, an easy game, nothing to worry about. They could have managed alone, without supervision. In fact they had already begun. They were indeed at the start of the second half and my boys were winning thirty-three to seven. How the hell did the Inveruno score a try?

It was towards the end of the match that the situation happened. We were five meters from the goal line and Gerardo, who was carrying the ball, started running in the wrong direction. He was chased by Giambattista and, behind him, a horde of opponents. Gerardo was agile and quick on his feet, but he was almost encircled. Giambattista tackled him ten meters from our goal, the ball flew away and the opponents scored undisturbed. The two were beating the crap out of each other and it took several minutes before we could separate them.

"What the fuck are you doing?" I cried, reaching them.

"He told me I was a deaf and dumb shit eater," said Giambattista.

"It's not true!" retorted Gerardo.

"I heard you, what do you think?" said Giambattista, "you were right beside me!"

"SILENCE!" I cried out. "Gerardo, tell the truth."

"Even if I had said something, which frankly I don't remember, how did he hear that? He is deaf-mute!" He was not wrong. We turned, all watching Giambattista.

"I heard him just fine!"

"Giambattista can speak!" shouted Antonio, "It's a miracle!"

What the fuck, was there an epidemic going on? First Filippa and now Giambattista. It was necessary to pass the thing under silence otherwise we'd end up in the evening news. The Bishop would ask questions. For that week, at least, I had to remain the grey man, anonymous, no attention whatsoever.

"I'm sure there's a plausible justification ..." I said.

"It's a miracle!" shouted Leonardo.

"OH! BE QUIET! I'm asking the questions here. Giambattista, can you really hear?"

"Of course."

"Since when?" around me everybody was quiet. The opposing team were approaching to understand what was going on. The referee was watching the clock and whistled the end of the game.

"I don't know, a few days ago, why?"

"What have your parents had to say about that?"

"I don't know, I told my mother that I could hear, but she was watching *A place in the Sun* on telly and she told me to go to my room. She didn't even notice. And then at home I never talk anyway."

The words came right out of his mouth without any impediment. What the fuck was going on?

"As I said, there's a simple explanation. The other day you clashed against Tommaso. Maybe it's due to a head injury, the blow has stirred something in the brain and now everything works as it should. Those are the mysteries of science, we only use ten percent of our brains, some kind of mechanism has been unleashed as a result of that injury. Come on, go get changed, and especially stop with all that bullshit about a miracle. Who is the priest here?"

Silence.

"I SAID, WHO IS THE FUCKING PRIEST HERE?"

Finally they said loudly and in chorus, "YOU, FATHER VENANZIO," like good Marines.

"Well. Get the fuck out of my sight, then. See you on Wednesday. Good victory, by the way."

Peter arrived at seven o'clock moving directly towards the wine rack, now reduced to a pittance. He got hold of a bottle of *Cavalli Tenuta degli Dei del 2012* and uncorked the bottle without asking for permission.

"I told her, you know?"

"Well done you. We must celebrate the good news, why not uncork a bottle of the good stuff? Ah no, I see you've already done it. You said what to whom?"

"I told Filippa who I really am."

Stupid idiot. Where did he learn all this honesty from? Certainly not from me. The South Africans had it right, in the past. Apartheid. Zero civil rights and freedoms. *I couldn't leave you alone for a moment that immediately you dug a hole for yourself.* "And what did she say?"

"We kissed, Venanzio."

Gosh, we reached the kissing point. And I was worried about having shagged a nun, after she was tortured by a Russian whore. "How romantic."

"No, I'm serious. I just didn't feel like I could lie any further. I took courage and told her everything. When I was at Oxford, the troubles after, and how I was deported to Nigeria."

"So she knows you're an illegal immigrant."

"Yes. She said that it doesn't matter. Venanzio, after what happened, that miracle, Filippa is a new woman, with lust for life and she does not care about what may be obstacles between us. She says she would be even willing to live in Nigeria. She makes a living by writing, and that you can do it anywhere in the world."

"Peter, wake up! You escaped from Nigeria at the first opportunity. And how do you think she'll react when you invite her in your Uncle Tom's cabin, with walls made of mud and leaves as ceiling?"

"You are an arsehole!"

I knew how it would end. Two weeks off in Africa and then the novelty would wear off.

Filippa would realise the harsh reality of certain places and would run like hell. In the meanwhile, my partner and semi-slave would have returned to his homeland. I filled the glass of wine and then I poured another shot for Peter. *Then He took the cup, gave thanks and gave it to them, saying, "Drink from it, all of you. This is my last bottle of good wine remaining, which is poured out for many for the forgiveness of sins.*

"I like this wine," said Peter.

"Enjoy it. Once that is finished, the only remaining bottle is a *Cancarone delle Murge*, denser than petrol. With a litre of those, the French would cut at least ten bottles of their Château Something."

"What happened to that jacket?" I asked, pointing my finger on a large patch of oil.

"Oh, this? Nothing, we were moving books and someone forgot a bottle of chestnut oil on the shelf. It spilled on me. Perhaps the old Baldacci was a painter in his spare time, as well as collector."

"Chestnut oil, you said?"

"Yes, I'm sorry about your jacket," said Peter.

"No worries, who cares?"

"What's to eat?"

"Salmon marinated in sweet and sour sauce and frozen in vodka as appetizer, lamb chops Villeroy style and finally a pear tarte tatin. Today the *perpetua* was in the mood."

"Come on, get the plates out, I'm hungrier than a hyena."

I went to the kitchen to get the dishes. Peter was quaffing the wine as if there were no tomorrow. Maybe he was right.

"Listen, I'm not saying anything more about this story of Filippa. You are a grown up and you do not need advice. I'm just asking you to help me out Tuesday, with that business about the Bible. Then I swear I won't engage you in any other businesses."

He did not think it over too much, he said alright without complaining, asking for money or grumbling. I lost him, I knew it.

By the time we were eating the second course we had attacked the bottle of *Cancarone*, but drinking it with those delicacies prepared by the *perpetua* was a crime. I was already half drunk and that night I had to plunder the Baldacci's house, I had to find a way to get rid ASAP of Peter. There was always the possibility that he ended up in trouble: the old ladies had a mountain of cash at home, and Filippa knew that Peter was an illegal immigrant. Once the money was gone, Peter would have been the primary suspect. If he had kept his mouth shut instead of being honest with Filippa, perhaps he could have avoided some trouble. After all I was fond of him. But by then the damage was already done.

I went back into the kitchen and took the water jug, a huge terracotta pot, gift from a faithful, I forgot who.

"Behold, a little fresh water will clean up our minds," I said laying it on the table. It was time to serve the tart tatin.

"Ouch, I am shocked," said Peter.

"You also buy your clothes at the local flea market?" I asked from the kitchen.

"No, I have my own stylist, it's called Caritas. At least when I don't dress in the clothes belonging to some deceased. Not bad this spring water of yours, it tastes like *Amarone della Valpolicella*."

"Are you already drunk? What the fuck are you talking about."

"Of course I'm drunk, taste it for yourself."

In fact the jug was filled with red wine. I poured a little in my glass. It was *Amarone della Valpolicella*, without a shadow of a doubt."

"STRIKE THREE," said the voice of God.

Three what?

"THREE MIRACLES. FUCK, DO I HAVE TO EXPLAIN EVERYTHING TO YOU?"

I guzzled down another glass of *Amarone*. What the hell was he talking about? Maybe Peter was God speaking to me? No, God I knew from before. Maybe Peter was the one who made the miracles. No, wait a minute, he was present at Filippa's one, and here with water and the wine but at the rugby pitch he was not there. Fuck I was dizzy. Peter, seeing me, took me by my arm and made me lay down on the couch. Then there was nothing.

CHAPTER 24

Tuesday, breakfast at Bulgari. OK, it wasn't breakfast at Tiffany's but neither were we in New York.

I had been up early to avoid the traffic on the ring road and getting into the city centre at a decent time. I woke at five AM. Peter wore a pinstripe suit that belonged to Giacomo Rossi, renowned roofer in Bareggio, known for walking around on Sunday dressed like a 1920s Chicago gangster. The original two-tone shoes belonging to the deceased were of the wrong size, unfortunately, so Peter wore a pair of black, anonymous shoes.

"Nice place you got here. If I am reborn I wanna be a Catholic priest," said Peter looking around. The entrance was sumptuous, modern.

"Are you guests here at the hotel?" asked a waitress watching us looking at the menu.

"No, business breakfast. Could you find a table for my colleague, while I do an errand? Possibly overlooking the entrance. We are waiting for a client and we would like be sure to see him when he arrives."

"No problem."

I went to the front desk. "This is an urgent

letter for Father Gregacci. Please deliver it by hand as soon as he comes down to have breakfast."

The envelope contained a postcard, nothing more, the only purpose was to locate Gregacci so to be sure when he wasn't in the room. Whoever it was that walked into the restaurant with a red envelope, that was our man, impossible to miss.

"So, are we clear with the plan?" I asked.

"You have killed me by how many times you have repeated it," said Peter.

"Better to be safe than sorry. Then, when Gregacci arrives, you'll have about twenty minutes to act. The room is 212; you go in, and turn everything upside down. If there's money there, you can keep it. But the important thing is that it has to appear as if a burglar visited the place. Turn the mattress upside down, throw down the desk and floor lamps, open the drawers and drop the contents into the middle of the room."

"Of course."

"Then there's the Bible. Grab the one I gave you in the briefcase and put it on the floor, as if a thief had knocked it over, careless of its true value. Stick the real one into the briefcase and get out of here."

I would have liked the Mission Impossible soundtrack in the background, but that was too much to ask.

"And how I am going to open the door in the first place? In your jaw-dropping plan you forgot to explain that insignificant detail."

I snorted. "With your black magic wand, of course. Here," I said opening my wallet and passing him an expired credit card. "You stick this between the jamb and the door. The hotel rooms have all the same locks, it is enough to use a bit of leverage and the door opens. I'd teach you how to pick a lock, but now we live in modern times, the hotels all have electronic locks."

Peter took the card in his hand, he weighed it for a while and then put it in his pocket.

"All clear? Hold on! Here. That's our target. Go to the elevator and then go to the second floor. I'll take off before he looks around too much. He may recognize me when we meet with the Bishop. I would say, we synchronise watches, but with the fake crap that you sell, there is little to synchronise. Twenty minutes, no more, and then you disappear."

"Aye, Aye, General."

Peter walked toward the elevator and towards the exit. One hour till the appointment with the Bishop, we had to discuss a few things before the arrival of Father Gregacci.

"Good morning, Sister Germana," I said.

"Good morning, Father Venanzio." Better to stay on the professional side, I was due to see her during weekend anyway. It was hard not to think about those two big tits and that arse of hers. "The Bishop is waiting."

A message on my mobile phone. It was Peter. I ignored it. Then another message, this time from Simonetta.

I found an idiot. By the way, I'm not pregnant, false alarm. You, however, are still an asshole.

She was not wrong. "Sorry, Sister Germana, what did you say?"

"You can enter," she said motioning me toward the oaken door.

"Father Venanzio, come, sit down." What the fuck was going on? Usually he was always mad at me, complaining that I wasn't doing my job, that I hadn't squeezed enough money from the parishioners with offers, and so on. "What is this story about miracles in Bareggio?"

"What miracles?" sometimes it was better to play dumb.

"Are you kidding me? The woman who

started to walk, the deaf-mute who can now hear and talk. Look, they even posted a clip on YouTube. Here, the Bareggio rugby club, is that not the team that you are training?"

"Yes, of course, but from here to say it was a miracle it is a stretch. We need to check the facts..."

"Venanzio, ride the wave, it's all publicity for the Church."

I wasn't sure I wanted to do it. Thankfully he wasn't aware of the water turned into wine. Now, that could have been a good plan B: set up winery, there was no need to cultivate grapes Laying my hands on a tank full of water and the game was done. Although a little voice told me it wouldn't have been so simple.

"We'll see. By the way, tomorrow I will deliver the App. We can put it online during the weekend ..."

Another message from Peter, which I ignored.

"I mentioned it in the Vatican. They support the project but they said we have to remove the component about the plenary indulgences. It would be a bad advertisement. You know me, I am always inclined to new lines of business, but unfortunately, I have superiors also. So, that feature has to go. Otherwise everything was accepted."

"I'll talk to the programmers, but I don't think it will be a problem."

Someone knocked on the door.

"Come in, Father Gregacci, please. Please meet Father Venanzio." And again! He never used my surname.

"My pleasure. Then, about this Bible from Grusch?"

"Here it is," I said opening the briefcase and putting the book on the desk in front of the Bishop. "If you want to examine…"

"Of course!"

Gregacci wore a pair of white gloves, picked up his copy of the Bible from his own bag and put them next to each other. He watched the details with a magnifying glass, touching, sniffing. In the boredom of the moment, I went to check the messages on my mobile.

The first was from Peter: *I can't open the door.* The second said: *twenty minutes gone. Bible not replaced, I repeat NOT replaced.* The third: *Gregacci is exiting the hotel. You're in trouble. Get out of there!*

No, I wasn't in trouble, I was neck deep in shit. They say that when one dies, one's life flashes before one's eyes like a movie. I was seeing the two hundred thousand euro flying away and exiting by the window.

"Hmmm, let's see what we have here ..." said Gregacci leafing through the pages, analysing. After a half hour of mumblings finally came the judgment.

"It is original, no doubt about it. Exactly equal to the Vatican copy."

"Are you sure?" said a voice. I realised later that it was me talking.

"Of course, no doubt about it. If my services are no longer required, I would return to Rome..."

"Thanks Father Gregacci, said the Bishop and the priest put his precious volume back into the bag and walked away.

It wasn't another miracle, of that I was certain, no electric shocks. Yet Peter had failed to replace the Bible. I did not believe in miracles, what I believed in was Occam's razor. The simplest explanation was that the book that Gregacci had brought was a fake too. It was easier to think that they didn't have it checked with the same care demonstrated by Benjamin. Maybe they've had it in the Vatican Library for twenty years and no one had bothered to do a detailed analysis recently. The good news was that the Bishop was now convinced of having an original.

"So, we said two hundred thousand euro?" said the Bishop.

"That's right. Here's the bank account on which you want to transfer the money." I passed a slip of paper with the details of my current account.

"Ah, a Swiss bank, great choice, trusted people." He turned on the computer and began to pound on the keyboard. "That's it, Venanzio. The transfer is done. I trust they will be happy to leave the Bible here while awaiting confirmation?"

"Sure, no problem. If you do not trust the Catholic Church ..."

When I left my legs were shaky. Two hundred thousand euro. I would give the Baldaccis a couple of thousand euro, the estimated value from Benjamin, considering the fact that it was a fake, even if exquisitely made.

I was an honest person after all.

CHAPTER 25

Riccardo had sent me the source code for the App, along with the greetings from Father Marcello.

I looked at the phone and I couldn't make my mind up, and yet it was a golden opportunity. It was ages since I turned on a computer, especially after what had happened.

I mean I had been a computer programmer for a certain period of time. I wrote programs primarily for financial companies. The quantitative analysis was a hot topic: creating mathematical and statistical models that represented the financial realities and extrapolate data to conduct transactions on the stock market. Fifty percent of the USA financial transactions was based on quantitative trading. Computers talking to each other and making transactions. Some computers were smarter than the others.

It was at that time, at the height of my success, that the devil came to visit me.

I remember how it happened, it was a Tuesday and an invisible force made me walk toward the church. I could hear screams coming from inside and I hurried up, thinking about a burglary. Two men were fighting, one was a priest. He was not winning, that was clear. The man on top of him was beating the crap out of him, but the priest, instead of defending himself kept chanting in Latin. I understood lately he was doing an exorcism. I just thought of saving the guy, so I jumped on the other man and I immobilized him. It wasn't easy, he had some strength. The priest got up and instead of listening to me and call the police he kept chanting. We were stuck. After almost an hour like that the man relaxed, exhausted. We were at peace. But something stuck, the devil wanted revenge on me. The priest thanked me and said I was a good man. I knew I wasn't. Never heard of him after that.

Don't try to imagine the devil red, with horns and a pointed tail. It had been months of pure terror, there was no escape.

I remained all the time in my house, tormented by demons, not eating, losing weight and I didn't know against which wall I should have banged my head.

Those demons were with me every single day. They wanted something from me, that was clear, but I didn't know what. All that suffering had brought me to the brink of insanity. And beyond.

It is said that the devil does not show itself, because for just showing up he would have confirmed the existence of God. I had cursed both of them, every single day that came on Earth, rather than take solace. Needless to say I had lost my job, my house and my savings. Everything.

I couldn't touch a computer anymore. The demons would be triggered as soon as I warmed it up. I slept on the benches of the Sempione Park and I walked around with a supermarket trolley, and a stubble. My only assets, some dirty clothes, a pair of military boots and a sleeping bag.

The food was not a problem, it had never been. I spent the evening at the back of restaurants and someone would always toss some food at me. It was not having a purpose in life or means to achieve it what was killing me. I had been taken away from the only thing I knew to do decently. When you're surrounded by devils all day, whom do you ask for help?

When I reached rock bottom, it was then than I heard God for the first time. Maybe I would have never become like that priest I had saved, but aiming at that was something to live for. A goal. I didn't really succeed.

I turned on the computer.

Silence.

I type the password.

Silence.

I opened the program from Riccardo.

A nice code, linear, well formatted. It had its own elegance, with indentation in the right spots. Thank goodness.

Once I had met a programmer who did not indent. All code was written left-aligned, and he used names of motorcycles and cars to program variables. If Ducati > = ref. Suzuki_GSX then Goto Lamborghini.

I was not in favour of the death penalty, but for those who used the "go to" instruction I made an exception.

The part that interested me was the code that managed the payments. There was a standard function to reach the banking system. That was pre-compiled, but it was going to be changed nonetheless.

For the first time in my life, I would do everything I hated in programming: no indentation, the most unlikely names variables, subroutines, references to left, right and center. A mess. And in between that puzzle, hidden, a small homemade program. Like hell they would find it. I thought it over for years. When I was a homeless man, I did not possess a computer but nobody forbade me to program in my head. "I saw" code, I could improve it, manipulate it, debug it, test it. All in my head. That was a miracle, Fillippa walking again was a joke in comparison. A slender, lightweight code, hidden, no errors. A true masterpiece.

I started writing on the keyboard and immediately the room caught fire. There were flames everywhere, the heat burned my flesh. Then from the walls came the demons. I was holding my head in the hands, I screamed, I couldn't move.

You are ours, they said. They revolved around me but I couldn't put them into focus, as soon as I placed my gaze on one of them, he faded like mist in the sun. The fire burned me, I felt my hands blazing. They were there, they told me every single sin I had committed. I was ready to go to hell, they said. They knew everything about my life, there was no secret I could keep hidden, not even the most intimate thoughts, and they spat in my face all the miseries and indignities to which I had taken part.

I started writing, slowly, I couldn't, come on Venanzio you are already in hell, go ahead.

Row after row of code I continued and I was burning. I wanted to scream, run, but where? I would not quit.

When needed, the voice of God was never around. God give me peace, blast me now and let me die in this instant! My sight was clouded, the tears ran down my cheeks but my fingers continued to write code as if they were independent. God what a torment, write, Venanzio, write, don't listen, they can't kill me and if I don't kill myself, I win. Write, declare, here, you see that the program is taking shape. Type, type, type.

Am I lost? Am I already in hell? No matter, continue to write, don't stop. I should have confessed how I beat Zambrini, maybe they were right. Write, Venanzio.

I would have thrown everything away, kill yourself now Venanzio, they will never let you alone, you cannot live like this.

And then it was nothing.

Peter woke me up that night. I was unconscious and sprawled on the floor.

He shook me up.

He shook me again, "Venanzio, wake up what happened?"

" I don't know where ..."

"Venanzio you passed out, you are burning

hot."

Peter was just one of the voices around me. The flames were gone and with them the heat that burned my skin, but the demons were not gone, they were still around there, they told me that Peter could not save me, I would die. I couldn't see, everything was indistinct, blurred, the room spinning around. "Peter, tell me, are you God? You'd tell me if you were, wouldn't you?"

" What the fuck are you saying, Venanzio, are you drunk?" I hoped I was drunk.

"Peter. I'm okay," I lied. "Look at the computer tell me what you see." Peter did not understand. "Tell me what you see on the screen!"

"Nothing, Venanzio, there's only the mail, here, you sent some files to someone, wait I'm searching. To the Bishop." Did I send the program then? I was able to finish it? I didn't remember. *Drink Venanzio, lift up your head, another sip.*

I sat back on the floor, I felt Peter pulling me by the arm, then he lifted me up and placed me on the couch. The room continued to spin around. Was I able to finish the program? I didn't know, I didn't have the strength to watch, I feared that the flames would reappear.

I closed my eyes. The dark, and noise were fading after hours of torment. I was tired, I couldn't do it anymore, no energy in the body. I could hear Peter but I couldn't understand what he was saying. The darkness was taking me, I lost consciousness.

CHAPTER 26

Almost a month had passed, a month!

Two weeks spent in my pyjamas, in bed, second degree burning and a couple of demons that didn't give up entirely. I didn't attend mass, I barely ate, I didn't do anything. The Bishop knew about the situation I was in, and for once he wasn't being a bastard as usual. On the contrary, he was delighted: with the new App for the faithful he had a new source of income and those in the Vatican had praised him. The Pope himself had called him back to Rome briefly, to congratulate him in person. A true defender of the faith.

What they didn't know was that the extra code that I added was a little naughty. A certain amount of donations from the faithful was diverted into a bank account in the Caymans on my behalf. In the agreements we had made for that App, any changes had to go first by me and by Riccardo for review, part of the contract. No one would have removed that program which was sucking money out of the Vatican account. Before it even reached their account, to be precise. And the users wouldn't have noticed. They were using an App of the

Catholic Church, so when they made a donation they were confident that the money would go to the Vatican, nobody would have dreamed of checking otherwise. My algorithm was simple but effective, a certain percentage of transactions simply disappeared and ended up in my account, neither the users nor the Vatican would have noticed anything. And even if they were noticed, trying to make enquiries on a Cayman Island bank would be a challenge. Those people didn't even reply to a magistrate.

I turned on the phone and looked at my bank statement. Not bad. I should have gone back to my duty, but not that week, the faithful could go to hell, they knew the mass by memory anyway.

Instead, my doctor came to see me.

"How are we doing Venanzio?"

"How are we doing, I'm feeling shit!"

"You had a psychotic event, it will take time."

Psychotic event my arse, I looked at my arm, at the blisters left by the flames in that room and I knew what happened to me. He looked too but he could not explain all those burns so he kept quiet. Instead, he gave me a prescription for painkillers. Good boy, better not asking if he didn't want to hear what I had to say. Maybe he was scared too about hell.

"I understand." I didn't but in that moment, I didn't give a shit.

"At least with those pills you will feel less pain. But stick to the dosage, it's strong stuff, you could get addicted."

Exactly what I needed. A thief and a druggie. There was a future for the Catholic Church. Doctors weren't much better, they were sorcerers, no more nor less than us priests. Warlocks who kept going by trial and error. I knew what had happened to me, I would have killed myself if that day I didn't ask for God's help. Why he decided to listen I didn't know. I knew I wouldn't be able to explain, I knew what I was saying didn't make sense, if you talk to God it's called praying but if God is talking to you, you are nuts.

"I want to return to live by the sea," I said. I didn't know how I got that idea, but I was certain that I would find some answers.

"A good idea," he said. He couldn't give me a prescription for that though. I knew, I asked.

"I know, I remember. But it's something I have to deal with. "

"At least you also hear the voice of God," said the doctor, "in your field that might be considered a bonus."

On another occasion I would have burst out laughing, maybe I would find the funny side in a month or two, but not right then.

He gave me a prescription for some other tablets, a cream for my blisters and I thanked him. It was time to leave, I'd see him again shortly anyway. The call from the Bishop arrived shortly after.

"Good morning, Father Venanzio."

"Good morning his Holiness."

"His Excellency is more than enough, you never remember, do you? How are you today?"

"I'm sort of feeling better," it was true, but I didn't want to appear too fit.

"A bad situation what happened to you. Listen, I'm calling you because we are forming a commission to investigate the miracles that happen in your parish."

Shit! "Is it worth it? It's not that then there was a proliferation of miracles, just three events that were a bit out of the ordinary."

"Three? Was there a third one then?" he said raising his voice. Christ, my big mouth.

"I meant two. You know I'm still confused. "

"Oh, okay," this time the Bishop seemed a little disappointed, "it doesn't matter, but we still need to do some basic checks. Do you know that the App is a portent? We had already twenty million downloads worldwide, if things continue to go smoothly, they will surely make me Cardinal before the end of next year."

"And then maybe you could be the next Pope."

"Maybe, maybe," Ah when the imagination runs free. No way of stopping it. Give us the chance of a career and we are not rational anymore. "By the way, as a reward for that App, I'm going to send you for a month to Riccione."

"To Riccione? But it wasn't where you promised to send me unless I reached the quotas for the quarter?"

"Ah yes, Riccione as permanent seat is torture, a punishment. But for a single month is a holiday prize."

If he said so. "When do I have to leave?"

"Next week."

"HERE WE GO. YOU WANT TO LIVE BY THE SEA AND YOU GOT IT. GO," said the voice of God. "GO TO THAT SHITTY PLACE OF RICCIONE, WHERE THE SEA IS NOT DEEP AT ALL. NO EFFORT IN SPLITTING THE WATER THERE."

"I obey. Look, as you know I'm not really in

good shape, on the contrary I feel terrible and I fear a relapse. I wouldn't like to be alone in Riccione, without a friendly face, if you know what I mean. I'm still recovering."

"Let's see," said the Bishop "let me think. Behold, I think here we have Sister Germana, who served for some time in a hospital. Do you remember her?"

I remembered, no question there!

"I'm not saying she would act as a nurse, you don't need one, but as you say, a friendly face in certain situations can be comforting. She could come with you."

"You are too generous, but I accept the offer. Praise the Lord."

"May He always be praised."

"Oh, one last thing. There is one thing that is very important to me, if I may ask."

"Of course, Father Venanzio. I am a humble servant of Christ, but if I can help out ..."

I told him what I had in mind.

"A conversion? Of course, you can count on me."

"YOU SHALL NOT MAKE FOR YOURSELF AN IDOL IN THE FORM OF ANYTHING IN THE HEAVENS ABOVE, ON THE EARTH BELOW, OR IN THE WATERS BENEATH. YOU SHALL NOT BOW DOWN TO THEM OR

WORSHIP THEM; FOR I, THE LORD YOUR GOD, AM A JEALOUS GOD, VISITING THE INIQUITY OF THE FATHERS ON THEIR CHILDREN TO THE THIRD AND FOURTH GENERATIONS OF THOSE WHO HATE ME, BUT SHOWING LOVING DEVOTION TO A THOUSAND GENERATIONS OF THOSE WHO LOVE ME AND KEEP MY COMMANDMENTS," said the voice of God.

No doubt I had a Caveman among my ancestors, a pious one, I thought.

"SOMETIMES YOU ARE SUCH A DORK," said the voice of God.

Thank God, thank You, I started missing you.

On the desk I had the contract to redo the rugby field, twenty-five thousand euro. I signed it and put it in an envelope, the guys deserved it and I would send the contract out in the afternoon. The clip on YouTube of Giambattista, miracle rugby player, had reached a million views and I had received a few calls from premier leagues teams, trying to land a contract with him. I had no objections in that regard; I had talked with his parents and agreed; the only condition that I had imposed was that Giambattista finished his studies. He could go and do training with the chosen major league team, even play on Sunday, but the whole thing was subject to his achievements at school. No school, no rugby. All parties agreed, I was just hoping they kept their word. Anyway, I had the managers phone numbers, I could check from time to time. Maybe in a couple of years I could put in a good word for Gerardo also, if that knucklehead had learned to keep his mouth shut.

There was one more thing to do before I left for Riccione. I dressed and went outside in the street, my old car was waiting for me. There wasn't much traffic luckily, my head was still spinning a bit and I didn't feel very comfortable driving. Luckily there were the back alleys, which took me to Pero within half an hour. At the address marked on the receipt there were only warehouses and factories. I parked next to the number written on the piece of paper, I got out of the car and I looked around. There was nobody there. The door in front of me was locked with a rusty padlock. I tried the key I had found in the Baldacci's library, near the fake Bible: the lock opened.

I opened the door hoping for a warehouse crammed with cigarettes and instead it was a bit of a disappointment. The space was not large, seven meters by five, some workbenches, one covered with a cloth, two chairs, a lounge chair, an old refrigerator. Sparta reborn in the Milan hinterland.

I checked, no beers. At the back of the room an oven, a shelf with brushes of all kinds, colours, oil flasks. It might have looked like a painting studio. I picked up a small bottle and read the label, chestnut oil.

I moved the towel and I found myself in front of a show: at least ten Bibles similar to one I had sold to the Bishop. I opened one, then another. My legs were shaking so I sat on one of the chairs next to me. *Well done Mr. Baldacci you found a hobby*, I thought. Other than smuggling, judging from what Benjamin had said to me, the fake Bible first appeared some twenty years ago. Then another at the Vatican. Who knew how many he had made in a couple of decades. *Not many*, I thought, those I had before me were dusty and under a cobbler, even with a lot of practice he couldn't make more than one per year. It meant that maybe there weren't many other Bibles like that out there. Good for me.

I examined all the Bibles, perfectly equal. Only three were not complete and had not undergone any treatment, indeed they looked new. Seven Bibles, two hundred thousand euro each totalled almost a million and a half euro. If I had sold one every three or four years it would top up my salary nicely. Too bad the old Baldacci guy had kicked the bucket, we could have been friends. I was sure of that.

I loaded everything in the car, Bibles, oils, brushes, about twenty paintings that I found on a wall behind another tarp, other books. I would have looked at everything calmly afterwards.

I also bought a bike. Used but well kept.

If the demons were now gone, I now had a song stuck in my head: *Hit the road, Jack.* Finally I bought a Triumph Bonneville, I didn't dare to go the full Monty and buy a Harley.

It was time to leave for Riccione. *And don't come back no more.* Well, at least for a month.

I was loading the poor bike with loads of bags, the rest would go into a backpack. The Triumph Bonneville, so reminded me of *La Poderosa* described by Che Guevara and Alberto Granado in the *The Motorcycle Diaries*.

I was almost ready.

It was then that I saw Peter coming, duffel bag on his shoulder.

"What are you doing here?"

"What am I doing? I come with you to Riccione, here's what I'm doing," he said laying the bag on the ground.

"And Filippa?"

"Maybe you were right, what kind of future can I offer her?"

"Did you talk to her already?"

"No, not yet, I don't have the courage. That's why I'm running away," he said, looking at the floor. Strange, Peter was hardly the type who would pull back.

"Wait here, don't move." I went into my office and picked up the envelope that I had left on the table. I had counted it to give to him before I left, but since he had bothered to come, I might as well get ahead of the times.

"This one's for you."

"What is it."

"Open it, and the mystery shall be revealed."

"A visa?" he said flabbergasted, continuing reading the letter.

"Of course. Commissioner Toscani himself pulled some strings with the ministry, he busted his arse to get it. Asking for favours, twisting necks, threatening. Ah, if someone asks, you are a political refugee, there is a second letter explaining everything, and you have just arrived in Italy. Stick to that letter as if it were the Gospel, pardon, the Koran, and everything will be fine. The rest you can find in the envelope. A bank account in Switzerland with a hundred and ninety thousand euro, the money earned with the fake Bible. If you're going to start a family with Filippa, at least don't start as a miserable refugee with patches on the back of your trousers."

"Venanzio, I ..."

"Get the fuck out of my sight now. Oh, and when I come back you have a job at the Church. It doesn't pay much, but between the money in Switzerland and the meagre salary maybe you can finish university here and take that degree."

"A job?"

"Yes, a real one, even if it is temporary. I expect you to bugger off as soon as you get a job on your own. The only thing you have to do while you're my employee, is pretend to be Catholic and to slave away. The latter shouldn't be difficult."

"I can live with that. Venanzio, I don't know how to thank you, I. .."

"I said, sod off. Go to Filippa and give her the good news. The sea awaits me."

"Beautiful bike."

"Indeed. You paid for it, I took the money

from the account in Switzerland."

"Arsehole, as usual."

"Yes."

"And with the miracles, how are we doing?"

Good question. "I don't know yet. For the moment I set aside the clothes from that flea market. No static, no miracles. When I come back, I will think about it."

"So we say goodbye?"

"For the moment." We'd meet again, I had no doubt whatsoever. If nothing else he would have come to me every now and then to suck the blood out of my wine cellar and snag a meal or two. I wonder if Filippa knew how to cook? Maybe she could have taken lesson from the *perpetua*.

I passed a cloth on the engine just to remove the last oil spots and the bike was finally ready. I looked at the rag, another sacred Shroud with a weeping Redeemer. You cry, you cry, you've walked through Israel, worked wonders, you got the fifty shades of Pilate, they crucified you but you didn't change us one iota. And maybe that was the point, at one point maybe you were so fed up with us and you thought, fuck! I take all humanity sins on my shoulder and you go and do whatever the fuck you want; you are all safe and pardoned. I wouldn't certainly start making philosophical arguments with myself. If God was working in mysterious ways, interpreting His will would have been impossible. Which amounted to not interpret it at all and not much would change, no matter how many Shrouds I found cleaning my sacred cock. Or maybe he was crying with laughter. From the top of his omnipresence, he knew that sooner or later some miracle would have gotten out of hand. And maybe in two thousand years, instead of kneeling in front of a crucifix, the faithful would have to kneel in front of a little Venanzio which was mounting a nun and stealing a Bible. I could already see the image, an altar, and on top of it a sculpture that represented me (blond hair) while I lifted up the skirts of a hypothetical Germana, busy sticking my sacred member between her legs. They would have had to review the part that said "let's exchange a sign of peace." Instead of shaking hands they would have shoved their hand into somebody else's pocket in an attempt to steal a wallet.

Or maybe it was all in my mind, and in that case Devils, God and miracles were the result of a hallucination, maybe even Peter and the Triumph Bonneville on which I sat. Difficult to judge, it all seemed so real.

So, why me? I asked.

"BECAUSE YOU CAN WORK OUT MIRACLES," said the voice of God. "BUT YOU ARE STILL SLOPPY, YOU LACK FINESSE, IF I MAY."

You may. So that's it?

"AND YOU ARE FUNNY. AND BECAUSE GOD, THAT WOULD BE ME, WORKS IN MYSTERIOUS WAYS. SO SUCK IT UP."

And that was it.

The only thing I knew was that I should have gone to Riccione. I knew that once there I would find some answers. It was time to leave.

It was time to hit the road, Jack.

THE END

Printed in Great Britain
by Amazon

25912607R00139